T0193873

Fate

THE BEGINNING

RODERICK HOWARD

iUniverse

FATE
THE BEGINNING

iUniverse books may be ordered through booksellers or by contacting:

iUniverse
1663 Liberty Drive
Bloomington, IN 47403
www.iuniverse.com
1-800-Authors (1-800-288-4677)

ISBN: 978-1-5320-6898-0 (sc)
ISBN: 978-1-5320-6899-7 (e)

Print information available on the last page.

iUniverse rev. date: 02/16/2019

I n remember the beginning but I can not see the end. All I see is the ride on the bus, shackled. Arm cuffed together and legs are to where I can't run and grab anything. Another place where people of the past say it's a cold stop. Nothing but guards yelling at you telling you to strip down naked so they can check for hidden illegal items and gang affiliated tattoos. Targeting the weak and want to make an example out of the strong. Yelling and intructing you to put on a jumper, asking for your size in sneakers, shirts, and pants so they could give you clothes in a bag later. Locking you into a cage amongst gangsters, killers, drug dealers and thieves. Another trip down a long hall accompanied by more yelling and insuls only to get locked into a 2 man cell with a person you may not know awaiting to get classified and shipped to your destination where you will spend the reminder of your sentencing time for the crime you have committed. Laying on the bunk with your hands on your head staring at the ceiling. Then closing your eyes and saying to yourself, not again. sighs....

THE BEGINNING

As a child growing up in a urban area that is congested with drugs, gangs, loud music, cars, and money is all you see. As a child it dosen't matter how people get money, all you see is popularity. People you would like to be like. The fame. The glory. The money. As you could see the fire hydrates blowing loads of water into the street people have turned on for you and your friends in the neighborhood. House parties being thrown and you setting at the top of the stairs watching. Listening to the music, watching girls dance exoticly. Beer and liquor getting drunk and white powder substances being snorted by some with clouds of thick white smoke in the air. Looking at all of this makes you feel like you are watching a rated-r movie your parents won't allow you to watch, but in the 80's-90,s it didn't matter. You remember listening to Marvin Gaye, The Isley brothers, Al Green, The Funka Dellecs inside the house and outside the house you heard Run DMC, Special ED, Eric B and Rakim, Slick Rick Doug E. Fresh, and many more. Especially NWA. Remembering your favorite movies like "Boyz N The Hood, Menace II Society, Juice, and Scarface that got all the attention of the locals. Wanting to be a rapper. Beat boxing as you watch Krush Groove. Wanting turn tables and rapping others lyrics like Big Daddy Kane. Just fun no worries. School you thought of as a place to hang out with your friends rarely seen on the streets because your mom wouldn't allow you to run the streets once you got home from school. She knew what was going on but you did not. Sometimes kids would make fun of you because you was one of the less fortunate ones to have stylish clothes or sneakers or your haircut wasn't right. That's a terrible feeling to get laughed at but wanted to fit in. Your parents didn't allow you to do what they could do when school was out. Their was a lot of killing going on that you never seen nor heard. Quite frankly you didn't know anything about people dieing or the people you wanted to be like in your local neighborhood was doing the killing. One day you was in front of your house throwing rocks across the street over a fence. Boys doing what boys do. Until a car drove past and everyone stepped back. You threw the rock hitting the passing car window. The driver gets out complaining and that's when for the first time you expressed your feeling of not caring for the first time using cursed words like "Fuck you." Surprising at the reaction you got from your mother and other family members asking where did you learn such words knowing you did not learn them from your mother. Scared because you already know that you are in trouble for throwing the rock you remain silent until your mother promises you will not receive consequences, your response is, you learned them from your father who did not live in the house with you and only go to see him on the weekends. Its more partying going on than you ever seen on in you mothers house. The x-rated stuff. You never tell what you see but mumbles go about amongst the family about your father to be true as you know it, but you liked it. On the very same day while sitting on your porch, which was on of your punishments for the moment, you seen your neighbor have a heated dispute and the result was a guy leaving and coming back with a baseball bat and beating him to the ground so bad his eye went missing. That was the first time you ever seen, but not the last to see somebody get hurt in front of you. Not knowing that your aunt was going out with the guy who was Puerto rican across the streets that has a brother as a big boy in the neighborhood. That story you will later learn about him. Your mother earns her living working in a factory and with six sisters and one brother they manage to move out of your grandmothers house and move two blocks up in a three bedroom house with two of her sisters not knowing the block that you moved on was the terittory of the most notorious gang called "The Sons of Malcom X" of North Camden which was the branch off of the "Junior Black Mafia" of North Philadelphia. Another notorious black gang that was only getting bigger. You was glad to been sent to the corner store because that's where everybody was, on the corner. Rapping, selling drugs, dice playing, nice cars, jewlery, the works. Sometimes you didn't come right back because you wanted to hang around them. Across the street was a chinese store who had a arcade in it where you and your friends would sometimes hangout at with a pool-house three doors down. Ninth & Vine was the best place you could live, as you thought as a kid. The local gangsters knew your name. Ask you favors for them and give you money that you had to hide from your mother. Then you started seeing your uncles from your dads side of the family hanging on the corner with the big boys, you thought it was awsome and it wasn't wrong for you to be there, In fact you use them as an excuse to be at the corner sometimes. After time past your sister would arrive. You was never jealous but happy because you got somebody to call sister and she was getting so much attention, you hanging on the corner watching things happen, your mother forgot about. Cool you thought. You remember going to your grand mothers house, your dads mom, on North 8th street visiting from time to time and traffic running in and out of her house like it was a conveinent store. You seen new faces all the time and money being given to to her. All you thought was whatevers going on it must be right grandma in on it too. They called her, the brick house. Once your mother and father had a fall out, not knowing why, you didn't see your grand mother because of the split up and as I said you would only see your father when he had time. Party, party, party lets all get wasted. That's the moto your father lived by. He was at every party. He was popular. He had many drinking buddies and a lot of girlfriends so you thought. He was the man in your eyes. Every time you and your sister would go see him is the time you would see house parties that you vow to never tell your mom. You seen grandma in action. You seen for the first time a gun but not the last. You never told anybody. It was your little secret. Now you curiousity come in about drugs and alcohol.

Money and girls. You never tried any drugs because you know your mother did not and would not accept it. So you didn't dare. Never upset mom. That's what you were taught. As the days go on you get more and more attached to your sister and the protection for her became crazy. One day you see another form of violence. An act that was committed by a gun that you have once seen. This is when big rims in wheels were popular. You knew people would always come out of the ally but not running scared. As you approach the ally riding your Big wheel bike a puerto rican man came running fast out of the ally towards you. He stopped because he didn't want to run in you turn around and started running the opposite direction but only to get stopped by a bullet that blow his brains all over the side walk. Scared and shocked at the same time because you never seen a gun fired before let alone see a man get shot by one. Watching a guy you knew and called fried died right in front of you. Hearing your mom scream running for your rescue because you were to scared to move. First time you seen a man die and surely not your last. School the next day as usual. Your mother is very strict on you going to the corner but she still ask you go to the store whenever she had money. You remember going to church and receiving blocks of yellow cheese and receiving paper food stamps. She is a victim of the struggle but refuses to receive drug money. She worked part-time at the factory to take care of you and your sister. With the help of your two aunts who lived with you was a big stress reliever. As time went on your clothes began to improve. Sneakers got more in style only when she could afford them. You use to ask yourself, why is these guys making so much money. Buying clothes, cars, and jewelry and live not so pleasant. Curiousity always come into play. Your two aunt moved across the street in two spate houses and that left you, your sister, and mother in the house alone. Your father was suppose to come and get yall every weekend but when they came no father showed up. Later finding out he has found another woman and began to raise his own family. That leaves you and your sister in the house on some weekend alone It was cool because you have your own friends on the corner that you did not look at as bad and you was growing up with friends that lived on the block as well. Summers were fun. Going to the local amusment park called, Clementon Park and going to Atlantic City to the beach. At these times your mother was doing a lot better being as though she was the only one actually raising you two. Single mother. She did it to the best of her ability. You go mom. Blocks of cheese and food stamps were still around but you knew mom made it happen no matter what. The strength of a mother you was being taught. As you got older you started catching onto what was actually going on on the corner. You started to hear from your friends mothers of how they were making two ends meet as street phamacudicals. You never seen your mother act in an unappropiete manner and made her living by working in a factory. You remember her bringing home donuts for you and your sister. Whenever October hit eggs were being brought and thrown

And houses set on fire every year. Sometimes the same ones. Everytimes you went to the corner or coming home school you would see a big spray painted picture of Malcolm X with his finger pointing, so big it took up the size of the house. Everyone knew the sons ran North Camden and I knew their intentions was to kill someone of their choosing to show heart and conpirisy. North Camden was so treachorus that if you didn"t live in North Camden don't come to North Camden. You could come in but it was sometimes to didn't come out. Rules of engagement you guess. As middle school really start to settle in you stated noticing there were different part of Camden. East, South Cramer Hill, Miguires, Pollock, Parkside, both Faiarview. The city each other. You also started notices different female in the areas. You middle school was mixed in with downtown people. Their were more Puerto Rican woman in which you are attracted to because your part of the city had more ricans in it. They called it little Puerto Rico. In this community you started meeting more friends. Your mother was happy. Your father wasn't their so you started latching onto more of your friends on the street. Six mother later your mother has met a guy later marring him and your life style started improving. Your mm got a job working as a mail carrier. Your step father in a computer technision working over Philly. As the two salaries combined your wants and needs started to fade. Birthdays and Christmases started to become better. Clothes and sneakers became better. On one Saturday you heard a couple of gun fires. You started to hearing more killings going on in your part of the city. You seen a car speed down the 10th street. You make nothing of it. You here in next morning that 2 people that you thought were cool were found in the back room of a house that was on Elm st. Two blocks in the back of you. One was killed in the back room and the other got found in the backyard because he tried to get away by jumping out the back window. One you remember because he use to walk down the 10th street and your street wearing headphone on his head. The other guy you remember because he use to hit on your neighbor all the time. You then remember going to stay the night across the street at a friends house you seen a guy get shot ten times on the corner. He was also cool too. Somebody you wanted to be like when you wanted to grow up. He was called out of the store to a pay phone only to arrive to a hell of gun shots. R.I.P. Eric. The next was somebody you looked at like a friend body got found around the corner in the park. It was shot, stabbed, burned and ran over. Wow. Everybody that you knew that died you have known to be associated with the gang. The message that the gang sent was serious. Mess with us and you get murdered. The cars that you seen everyday was point eight Toyota All colors Different interiors. Corola twin cams with baby supers rims on tires that were thin. Chevies and Buick Reguels sitting on rims. You remember going to every puerto rican parades that went on every year the last Sunday in June and the one in Philly was The last Sunday was in August so you thought. Your remember going to them they had live bands floating on large carts groups of cars all looked alike drove together in different packs. Loud music. Fire department spraying water on people. You have super soakers water guns being filled with water shooting them at each other. You even seen people jumping out of cars wetting who ever that they were at water battles against each other. You seen a gut named Chill Will having the loadest system in a Buick Regal in the whole Camden. Chains you seen like Slick Rick in his music videos. Haron bones been wored really wide. Cubin links chains. Females with all types of sneakers, purses, dresses, hairstyle. Nails done. Selling drugs was the way to get it if you wanted to live that lifestyle being sharped up to the tee. But when you messed up you knew they were going to find you died somewhere. You then learned that a person brain was actually was a different color that is installed in the skull of your head. Crazy what the streets show and tell you that the schools did not. You now go to school keeping up with the latest clothes fashion' Keeping up with the hair styles from tall box hair cuts to waves to gumbies. Pumps. The tail in the back of your lower head. Finger waves. Big ear rings. Big four finger rings. You were the class clown. Making every laugh. You would come to like the Puerto rican girls from downtown and in your neigborhood. After school you and the local neighborhood kids would get into fights with the downtown. Some would get on the bus and the others had to fight there way out of the city that were walking home. They later became your friends. Crazy how childhood friendships start. Some were scared and use to run while others would stay and fight because they knew that had to come back to school the next day. They earned their respect in your neighborhood. The same went on downtown. IF you wasn't from downtown you didn't belong in their. If you didn't have family that lived down their don't come there.

Especially East Camden and Miguier projects. The Acres out east. 32nd st. But in before you get into high school you didn't know anything about these other places that you could not go to because your high school was in another part of the city. What people didn't Know is that when you were home you was getting your butt whipped bad when your step father felt as though you did something wrong. Punishment was serious. You were scared more for the punishment was going to be if you got in trouble than actually doing he actual offense that was committed. As well as morals and respect was being thought inside of the home. Chores and responsebiltiy. Your stepfather was into culture. He reads a lot and knows about Black history. He was into black culture so much on one Easter he dressed you and your sister in African garmets. He enrolled you into sport programs like basketball, football, baseball, and boxing. Inside the home he was physically abusive. Whenever you got into trouble it was long beatings with yelling. He would beat you so long you would throw up from all the yelling followed by two weeks room punishment without a t.v. or a radio. Do you know how much belt whippings and yelling you would do in order to throw up? A lot. Summers you never got to enjoy because you was on punishment. Whenever your household family went on trips to amusement parks you would have to stat home on punishment alone. You stayed in your room so much that other parts of the house didn't matter and being alone you felt comfortable with. Enjoying outside activities you didn't care about because see or hear about them because you was always on punishment. No class trips. No vacations. You took up hobbies like model cars, boats. And planes. Started liking train sets and fish tanks. You had a 20 gallon fish tank filled with parhinas with encyclopedia you would read. So all you did was read and admire you fish. No girlfriends because you would be on punishment at the time. You had one girlfriend that live on the block next to yours who understood you and your punishment. It was time when your parents would go to sleep and you would stick your head out of the window and call your girlfriend in which she had the backroom at her house and she stay on the side where her back window was facing the same alley way that ran in the back of your house. So that was cool. You had a in school girlfriend in which you only seen her when you went to court. So it was the rican girls you were more attracted to. You started learning to speak spanish now and learning to dance all their dances. You were good at it too. Your girlfriend that live in the block behind you left to Germany when her mother found out that she was no longer a virgin. Her husband was in the army and stationed in Germany at the time. You were heart broken. You had lost your best friend. You didn't see her again for another five years. You learned how to stay focused on books because of your punishment so school was easy to you. You liked to read books and learn something from them. So going to school you went to everyday and your mom made you. You no long heard all the killing, fighting and drug selling. You were smart in school but wanted to be the class clown got you into trouble all the time. Every time you got off punishment you wanted to hang out with you friends and catch up on old gossip. You ran with your friends and chased girls. Once again doing what boys do. Sports is back in and the summers are here again. You always manage to maintain good grades and never got left back. You brung in a F every now and then but always completed your grade school year on time. Their was a girl that lived across the street and you liked her. She was light skinned with green eyes. She became you girlfriend for the summer. Your cousin went with her sister and your friend that lived across the street went with the girl next door. Yall all hung out together on the block. The other boys on the block became your childhood friends because you all stayed on the same block. Snow ball fights. Street football. Going to the basketball court together along with the other kids the lived in the area. Like around the corner or on blocks that were not to far from yours. Y the end of the 80's-1994 to 1995 the notorious street gang Sons of Malcolm X no longer was around because they either died or got locked up for selling drugs, gun possessions, or murder. Their reputation still lived in North Camden so as growing up you and your friends up held that name of being from North Camden. Their were Many abandon house because houses were being buried on October 31srt. Holloween. The biggest fire you ever seen was the chinese store on your corner. You didn't know why the store was on fire because that was the hang out with arcades in them and they made chinese food. The only chinese store in your neighbor hood. Your girlfriends parents were in the FOI movement. The priciples are different from the NOI, but still praised the same god, Allah. All praises do. Your girlfriend could not stop the physical abuse you were going through inside the home. She really didn't know because you was embaressed to tell. Afraid she would not understand. Everyday your mom would yell out the door for you to come in. Nine o'clock to be exact. Sometimes it was embaressing because your mother was the only mother doing it. Laughter came every once in a while but after awhile you would laugh too. Between you being on punishment all the time and going to school it took a toll on you relationship and it was soon to come to a halt. Another heart breakers. Do you know how that made you feel with missing summers anyway because of the long punishment. Sometimes you would get off punishment and get into trouble right away and you were right back in the room. Like you did not learn your lesson. Being alone so much and being segragated from the outside world like a cell, you became immune to it. It didn't bother you anymore. The whippings and going to school with whelps bothered you more than just being in the room all the time. At one point you would say to yourself I just got off punishment, would you think just a little talking to would help instead of cleaning up your own throw up. You didn't dare to talk to him like that though it would only make things worst. You even got a whipping the entire house heard because it was on Thanksgiving. He was mad because you touched the food without saying your grace. So embaressed you didn't want to eat with the family. High school in now and its a new girls. Older girls. Some your age but you know in high school you are mixed in with upper class people. This is the time your and your friends from North Camden was in somebody part of town. The tables turned. You now in East Camden in Woodrow Wilson high school. All people did was fight in and out of school. Now its you and your friends fighting your way out. Everyday it was a new battle. It was big group fights. You didn't know where the punches came from. Luckily you learn how to box along with past fights you had in the neighborhood Learning was not in. It was all about the fashion, girls, and fights. The fights were so big, the police be outside waiting for it to kick off. The girls use to fight too. You had to earn your respect from people in the other area of Camden. Some fights you end up being friends with while others you would become enemies. Sometimes the girls would come t school with cleats in their book bag. Ready. On go mood. Sometimes the fights would further esculate beyond school. You would make it home and gather up other from the neighborhood then go back to there parts of the town for round two. A u-haul truck was even rented just for a bunch of yall to get into a jump out on the other boys in their part of the hood just to let them know your part of the town was bigger and better. Reputations had to be upheld. Some East Camden boys didn't go to school just to arrive there after you get out. The Acres didn't like North Camden. Just like the miguier project didn't like the Acres but was cool with North Camden, but downtown didn't like North Camden for the fight they had to go through to survive and earn there respect. The city was wild. Their was a field right across the street from the school. Sometimes you would chase the boys over the park back to the Acres only to arrive to see the Acre boys were there waiting for you to come across the field. We felt we had to keep the North Camden name alive because we live in it as well. This is the time I really started to hear about the housing complex call "The Acres." Talk about the housing projects in New York. Well these were the same. You could get anything in the Acres. From drugs to money. Their were stash houses. Secret doorways. House in the top of the complex only those who live their knew about because whenever the police would chase you, you knew how to get away and the police would never catch you. They even would get lost. It was times when the police would not even go into the Acres. Kinda let people do what they wanted to do. Welfare was everywhere. Jobs were the drugs going in and out the Acres. They had a name they also had to be upheld. The police knew if they go in alone, They could be shot and don't know where it came from. Some of the most violent people in East Camden came from the Acres. So as we chase the other students across the field we would run into the boys from the Acres who had guns, bats bricks, brass knuckles you name it. They had holes in the walls where it looked like they were not even there. With a lot of police outside of school when let out, hey couldn't even stop the fights. Their horses used to smacked in their buts to make them jump or start running. It was like a war zone and we were all teenagers. The girls of North Camden could not be beat. Everyday they were ready. Sometimes more prepared than the guys. Ready to throw down with the guys if need be, but they had problems with the other girls too. Dudes from other parts of the city wanted to hook-up with them. The fighting turned on some guys. Knowing the chick you were dating could hold her own. This sometimes could not happen because they knew if you go into another part of the city even to see a girl it could be trouble. This is how it went down eveyday at Woodrow Wilson high school. You had the famous 32nd street boys who ran with the Acres. 32nd Street had a name for themselves as well. Goons for real. You also had the Miguires projects and the well known place called "Th Alley way." They took over the game and replaced a place call "The mailbox." Miguire projects were cool but when it was time to go down they ran with East Camden because that's where they were located but they were seprete. A place of their own. The Alley way was right across the street from them. Having access to all things also like guns and drugs. Anyone who dealt with the Alley way had money. Not a couple of hundred of dollars but thousands. So much drugs came out of there they had the police on pay role. They were a gang but a gang of people who protected it. So much money yahts were even bought. More into that later. In the middle of your high school year you got kicked out. Another school in the city told your parents that you could not be enrolled into their school because if you kicked out of Woodrow Wilson you were trouble. Camden high school enroll teenagers that lived in parts of the city of Pollock, Parkside, Centerville and both fairviews Woodrow Wilson had East, North and parts of downtown. You got accepted into Pennsaken Vocational school. Most of the Puerto Ricans from

Cramer Hill, North Camden, Downtown, and Fairview. So you stop getting into fights and got more into the girls. You noticed that not only was North Camden little Puerto Rico but Cramer Hill had a lot of Rican girls. You never would see them unless you were from Cramer Hill. You were in love with one particular female. She was beautiful. She later became your friend. The courses you took up was Carpenrty/Framing. This is what you wanted to do. Building things with your hand out of wood. With all the girls and learning how to frame houses and decks you went to school every day but it did not stop the crazy beatings you would get from home. Now you start smoking weed. Drinking a little. Hanging out now with people who did the same. All these things you felt you were missing because you was always on punishment. Started showing off for the girl. You had a sense of humor. All of your friends started to become more Puerto Rican. You started learning more Spanish and more dancing. The teachers started having problems with you acting out all the time. You were not a bad kid a was smart when it came to the school work. The teachers didn't understand why you kept action up. Misunderstood you thought. Your behavior towards authority was becoming a problem. You did not like getting told what to do. By the end of the school year the principle told your parents they didn't want you to come back to their school even though you past. Damn and you liked the school. Your sophmore year was a new beginning. You were enrolled into Sicklerville Vocational School. Now that school felt like heaven to you. 12 building with 10 being occupied by you and other students. You took up the same course. Building is what you loved to do. The number of other student were massive. Teenagers from all over not just Camden. Some teenager drove to school and some took the buses. At least 30 buses were in the parking lot. The school looked like a college campus. Their were so many girls there, you didn't see the same girl twice sometimes the entire school year. 2 cafertireas, and olympic size pool, and a very big gym. You loved it. Never skipped school. You flirted with every girl you seen. Every day was different but the fact remains you had to go home to your step-father you resent. You played football for the Centerville Simbus in the summer and played basketball. You also played baseball a lot. You ran track and field and you won metels and trophies all the time but didn't feel like a winner at home. Like whatever you did was not good enough. You had your sister to worry about but you were going through so much it was to much to bare. Besides your mother protects her. No one to stop him that will protect you. Lonely you felt. You learned more about your culture from him and at the same time you did enjoy different places when yall traveled out of state to see you aunts. With your aunts living in different states you learned different cultures as well. Different people. You went to Georgia, South and North Carolina, and New York. He had family in Baltimore. So that was cool always going there. You had family from Boston to Florida. When you needed help he was there. He was like Dr. Jeckel and Mr. Hyde. Recovering drug addict and now have it all together. There were times you did not want to go onto family trips and only wanted to stay home alone. Read books, workout, and learn more about fish. You learned to humble yourself. Look, listen, learn, observe, and respect. So you learn by watching and observing things in which you already knew because you saw them outside on the streets living on the block from the notorious street gang. You listened to all what they had to teach. It was right on your door step. You learned respect. Sometimes on the weekend you and your block friends would smoke weed and drink 4o's on the opposite corner of the Sons of Malcom X. You were starting to fall what society wanted you to become. Ghetto. A thug. A failure. Falling victim to drugs and alcohol. You were always different because inside of your household their wee structure and rules Morals and respect. Books and learning lessons. You grew up straight and had no choice. You had the best of both worlds. Inside the home and outside of the home. You didn't get into trouble that much on the street because you know your mother didn't play that and you didn't have that much freedom like your other friends had. Besides if you got into trouble you had to hear it from your step pop in which to rather not do. So you were cool. You just looked forward to school. Their were times when you got suspended. Imagine the butt whippings you got when you got suspended. 3 to 9 day suspended days at home. Your parents use to get so mad because you were smart and didn't understand why you were acting up in school all the time. It was embarrassing to your parent and your step pops didn't like it. Not the problems that you lost but making them feel like they were raising you foolishly. The teachers to the principles liked your step father because he was well mannered and they knew that inside your household it was stable and well placed. Both parents worked and yall did family outings. They didn't allow you to run the streets. A good home and you embaressed them every time you got into trouble. That's why the punishments were so harsh. You never got used to it and you still managed to pass every time the school ended. Not because you were of fear but because you were smart. School was fun with all the girls and you had a crew. It was 4 of yall. Cooling. Especially when gym was to come around. An olympic size pool and you had to take that portion of gym class. The gym was so big it was 4 different classes at a time in it. Freshman, sophmore, juniors, and senoirs. The teachers event liked you because you were social, respectful, and well mannered. Even though you were from Camden you were not like the rest they always heard about but never seen because they were not from Camden. They took advantage of that. You were not shy in class and didn't mine getting put in front of the class to either make a speech or to answer questions. You were funny which gave you leverage and you didn't run with the rest of the crowd. Your crew was about the girls and chilling and becoming popular because you guys stood out from the rest. No sagging your pants. Clothes were always new. Always kept a haircut. You all were one of a kind. Plus you all were in the same classes. You all graduated and on to the next grade. 10th grade now a sophmore. You and the guys are in the same trade so you are mostly to go to the next carpentry class. In the summer you always staying touch with your closest friend which was the hang out. His mom smoked weed. Your closest friend which lived in East Camden, One of your fiends who lived on 32nd st. Was always thugged out. Your other friend lived in Cramer Hill. We all would go to your friends house that lived in East Camden and chill in the basement to play his game system smoke weed and cigarettes. You all experienced drinking liquor and smoke cigarettes. Your friend that lived on 32nd st. Was already hustling drugs so he was in the mix of things. You all liked him. He was advanced when it came to the street life. He didn't care about anything. All of your first experinced with cigarettes was crazy. You got a stimulation from the smoke that you inhaled after smoking weed. You felt like it enhanced your high so you began to like them. It first hurted your lungs but as you progressed, it didn't hurt anymore. You all smoked weed until yall was incoherant. Your friend who lived in East and Cramer Hill played the NFL game Madden all the time. You sat back with one of his cousins who lived in the house but did not go to the same school as all of yall did. He was cool too. All around the same age bracket. He was smart. He was extra funny and intelligent. We all experienced the vodka. It became your favorite choice of drink. Coughing and the burn in your chest as the vodka went down after taking shots. You liked it though. It came with drinking hard liquor. Something you would then get use to. It ran in your blood because everybody on your dads side of the family drank even your grandmother. Your uncles always got locked up and sold drugs. That was the life at the time. The 70's and 80's were real as you knew it. You were into girls, liquor, beer, and parties. You and the guys use to walk from East Camden to North Camden to play the local guys in the neighborhood in basketball. You had you starting 5 against any other starting 5. You would set up the North Camden basketball event. Your friend from East would set up those events a. your friend from Cramer Hill would set up the basketball events in his part of town. All over you two was. Just enjoying life as a teenager. You two would just walk up to the court and challenge whoever. East was the hardest to play in. Those guys were good. They knew how to ball. You two would play sometimes until it got dark and the lights came on. It made you feel good. Made you feel like these were the things you were missing every time you would be on punishment 2 weeks at a time. Your friends felt bad for you every time but understood. You started to developed anger towards your step pops. Sophmore year sets in. You immeditely group up with your friends. Everybody stepped up a grade so everybody knew everybody. The girls seem like they transformed over the summer. School went the same jumping from bus to bus. Waiting all day for the gym class to start. Doing your work fast. So fast, when the teacher gave out homework, you would do it right then and their. You and your friend would walk the halls like you owned them. You would go from building to building to see all the girls you sometimes didn't see when you had class in one building. Now you began to smoke weed at the bus stop before school. You would go to school mello and more comfortable with going to school. Still felt alone and still had to go through the torment. You were getting bigger and your step pops would handle yu differently. More aggressive. More like you were already a man. Knowing you still had that fear in you, on one Thanksgiving day your whole family was at your house to eat. Food was on the table. The smells of all of it filled the whole house. Right before prayer were made before eating, you sat there staving. Craving to eat badly. You decided to touch the food before the blessings were made. Your step pops was so upset, he hook you upstairs and beat you so all would hear then sent you back down stairs. You gathered yourself and followed his intructions to go back down stairs. You sat at the table embarassed and your family did nothing to stop him. Not even a word to him. You would never forget it. Just like one time you got in trouble in school and you know that the school called home and left a message on the machine. You waited in fear until he came home. Once he got home he listened to the message he ordered you to strip down and put on your robe then come down stairs and grab to chairs. You would put one on top of the other with the legs facing up. He told you to hold on to them and if you would let go as he beat you it would be worse. Your mother sat and watched you as he beat you half crazy as usual and you already knew that you would not hold onto the chair and yes it would get worse. Until you threw up. Crazy. You would just look at your mother as you walked up the steps with the thought in your mine, why didn't you tell him to stop. The respect for him was now gone. You thought if love felt like that you would not want it. School went on as the same and once you were off punishment the phone calls came pouring in. You also had a computer at home so those began your daily routine. You daily chores were cleaning the kitchen and taking out the trash. Cleaning the bathroom came on the weekends. You would get allowance sometimes, but that was not the lesson. You looked going to school every day. You would go to school at times in pain from the previous butt whippings but you were not an angel all the time so it came with you growing up. You acted out. You acted out sometimes against other people. In the other house you thought it was cool. You just wanted to do what the other kids did. To the naked eye everyone thought the household was fine until it came down to the punishment. Then it was hell. At this time your mother gave birth to another child. It was a boy. A little brother. At that point you thought things would get better. You thought things would sharpen up with the relationship between you and your step father but it didn't. Your mothers marriage has gotten deeper and the bond now would get deeper. Despite what was going on inside the home, the mother son relationship would be better, but the feeling you had towards your step pops was different. Your mother never treated you differently and that was cool. You still felt the emptiness. That yearn for attention you wanted was no longer there. As long as your mother was happy you didn't care. As time went on you gotten wiser. What not to do until one day you got approached by a guy you knew from down the street. He was way older than you. He asked you if you wanted to make money. You said yes. A chance to make money without your mom and step pops knowing. Why not you thought. So you and your friend got shown the way. The first day being as though you was new to the block was okay. You both felt like you were getting it off and you could see yourself doing this and not getting caught. Selling rock cocaine is what the next move was. You both looked out for each other. Until one day you seen your dad and step mother just so happen to be going to a guy to talk to him about getting their car fixed. The neighborhood mechanic. You never seen them on that street until that particular day. Your father seen you and pulled up to ask what you and your friend was doing in that area. You never gave him a response as you seen a customer was coming to confront you about a purchase. Your father knew what it was and as a parent he told you to leave and if he was to catch you again out there you will not live to see another day. Your father was about 6'-0" and weighed in at 250lbs. He was way bigger than you and your step pops and the fear you had for him was different. You never tell you father what was going on inside the household because you knew it would only upset your mother so you said nothing. That's the only person you did not want to upset out of all people. You went home scared because you thought your father was going to call your mother on the phone and tell her what he has seen but he never did. Once you got home for some reason your mom did not allow you to go back outside. You had the drugs on you in the house and knew if you didn't show up or at least give it to your friend to give to the guy or you give it to him yourself it was going to be a problem. You tried to force your way out the door and your mother fought you off leaving you with a scratch on your face that was deep enough that you were bleeding. That was the least of your worries. You knew once your step pops got home and she tell him what happen you were going to be in a whole world of trouble. You was downstairs when he came into the house. He went upstairs to greet your mother in which it was the time she would tell him what happened. He comes downstairs furious with you. So furious that you and your mother had it out that he threw a punch that knocked you straight to the floor. At this time you have picked up a few ponds and decided that you had enough with him putting his hands on you so you fought back in defense. Out of nowhere you wrapped your arms around him lifting him up and slamming him to the floor. You both was stunned at the action. More him than you. He just told you to go upstairs and you did so. From that point on it was tension in the house between you to like two grown men. To young to get kicked out but old enough for the physical abuse to continue. Never got big headed over the event but lived in fear that one day it was going to go down in the house not because of what you would do to get into trouble but because you was going to fight back. So you go to the kitchen to grab a knife to put underneth your pillow then between your mattress and the box spring. Why? Because you knew that one day after it was to go down you were going to go into your mothers room and stab your step pops. The reason why it never happened is because they slept in the dark and you didn't want to stab the wrong person. So you waited for one day he would slip up but that day never came because he found the knife underneth you pillow. He never questioned you on it but had a feeling why. Every day after that you would keep an eye on him. Walking on egg shells everyday knowing he was going to question you about it but he never did. Sometimes you would just stay in your room and read and watch tv. instead of going into the presents of him. Your room was your safe haven. No one bothered you in the room. Your young man cave. You would study your pirahnas. You had five of the in a tank. You would also read things inside of you encyclopedias. Researching and learning new things you were into. They were resourceful when it came to school essays and just looking up on things you did not know about but knew the names of or events. You became a good writer because your essays were written with feelings. So you would write, read, do essays, study, workout, and watch tv. to stay out of the way. They were like an outlet. The tv. and radio would get taken away from you because of punishment so they became unimportant to you. Just you and your creative thinking. You also picked up a hobby. Building model car, trains, planes, and boats. From time to time you would enjoy doing puzzles with your mother. Those days were nice. You liked to spend time with your mother. The bond became deeper. 1,000 piece puzzles when she had time because she had to tend to your little brother. It was cool to have a little brother. Seeing him walk and talk and how he took to you as a big brother. Now you as the big brother you had to look after both your little sister and brother. On your dad side you had two other sisters and a step brother who you looked at like a blood related brother. You were the oldest out of all of them. School was school. Every day you would smoke weed with one of your friends. You both would get to the bus stop earlier than the rest and smoke two blunt rolled weed. That's what they were called at the time. You brought some weed when you had the money and the other he brought. He always had money. In the beginning of every school day you were on cloud nine. Wrong but felt right. You couldn't hold down a girlfriend for two reasons. (1) was because what you were going through at home you knew she would not understand and (2) you were so flirtasious with all the girls. You liked them all. Their was one time you tried to hold down a relationship with a female from Cramer Hill. Everyone was shocked because you two was together but you liked her a lot. At times other people would see you two kiss in between classes in the hall and after school. One day you got time out after school to go see her. Nobody was at her house and you already knew what time it was. You both would go upstairs not to her room but to her mothers room. Not knowing why, you just went with the flow. You thought you was in her room. You were in the mood that she set. You liked her a lot so up for the moment didn't take hard to get their. She was leading the way. Normally you would but this time was a little different. Right before you would play on the bed naked her brother knocked on the door. He was bigger than you. He had respect in his neigborhood. It was not only him, he was accompanied by two of his cousins. In your mine you was like, oh no I'm caught in the house with no way out without confrontation with them. You both hurried and put on your clothes. When you both went downstairs her brother was shocked that you in the house and told you that you had to leave. He went outside first while you stayed in. Your girlfriend knew what was about to happen so she guided you outside. It was a good thing she went first because at the end of the walk way on the porch one of her cousins was standing around the end of the porch that you could not see but you saw the other on the outside of the gate. Once you got past the corner of the porch she attempted to stop her cousin from hitting you as her brother just sat on the chair like a boss. She told you to go but she could not hold him that long in which you had to approach the gate to get out of the yard. You came in counter with the other cousin. Now one is in the back of you and one is in the front. Crazy positon but you had to fight your way out. The one cousin threw a punch in which you weaved but only to get hit by the other from behind. They grab your shirt as you tried to fight and run away. You couldn't beat them both but you tried your best as you try to get away. With your shirt ripped, you manage to break free and run away towards your aunts house which lived a couple of blocks up. You got there safely and you step pops and his friend just so happened to be there. They asked what happened in which you told them out of state of shock. They put you in the car to take you home. You were so upset at the event, you called the relationship off with her the next day. It wasn't her fault but you felt embaressed and did not want to be put in that situation again. You still liked her and she did you as well but it could not go on so she was heartbroken. (sigh) So you go back to you flirting business. It is turning that you and your ways were like your fathers but you were still dealing with the tension inside the home in which it made you stronger. Your thoughts were deeper than the others because you always had time to think. Your approach with authority was civil but didn't like to get bossed around. A side effect of what was going on inside the home. No one understood as you think while standing alone. By the end of the school year your grades came back they were not at all great but the most important thing was that you got promoted. Another year down. Nothing has changed but you attitude towards things. As you get older you get smarter. Learning more about the African history and read more book pertaining to black authors. A different perspective on how you was being taught in school. Learning a different understanding about history. Learning that the things you were taught in school are not completely true. Your eyes start to open to different intel based on the insight you learn with the study of your culture. Different history. Those books you get from your step pops. He never denied you knowledge and out the books there so you can read. So you took them and paved your own way. Knowledge s beyond infinite. The summer comes into play and all activites start and you are in all of them. Neighborhood basketball was the thing you and your block friends did all the time. The basketball court was right around the corner from you. Theirs also a park called "Northgate Park" everyone goes to. It's in your area just a few blocks down the street from where you live. They use to have 3 on 3 tournament there. The YMCA use to host a lot of events there. They even had a hand ball court that you could play on both sides at the same time if you wanted to. They even hand a tennis court which was cool. They had monkey bars, swings, a big playground for mothers to bring their kids to. Even a sprinkler set up that would come on hot days. The park was nice. The older people who smoked weed would smoke all the way in the back by the barbeque pits. You also had another park in the neighborhood called "Pyne Ponte Park." That is where the local swimming pool is at with the lifeguards that everybody knew. They had an inside basketball court, gym, and a boxing gym. In the other building that they had have a recreational center in it. Kids can go play table tennis. The park was so big people use to bring the dirt bikes out. Moe pads, motor cycles and all types of bikes you can drive or ride. People would come out on the weekends with their cars lined up and play their music and play dominos. Drinking beer and socializing with others. Cooling and enjoying the summer outside of school. You didn't get into to much trouble because the summer was all yours. You had female friend and got more involved with the local Puerto Ricans who live in your area. You learned to speak Spanish and dance all the types of dances they had. You loved their culture. It was different from the music to the language to the women. School is back in and now you are a junior. 11th grade was different. You older now. You are now becoming the role models for the lower class men. You friend from 32nd street had a car so you now getting picked up and no longer riding the bus. At the end of the day you all would smoke weed on the way home. Extra high. He knew where to get the good weed. The other student are more into the streets and they sometimes brang the problems from home into the school but you were cool because they were your friends from Camden. Now you look forward to class trips that you never attended because you constantly getting into trouble getting suspended at times but school was fun to you. It made you upset because class trips were part of high school. You were still u to the same tricks. Kissing girls in the hallway. Jumping from bus to bus when you didn't ride in the car with your friend. All what they talked about high school you were doing. Regardless how you felt at home you always came to school with excitement. Looking forward to socializing with the girls. From Camden to other neighborhoods that was not from your area. The suburban girls. They were different. Got raised different. Not around all the violence that were going on in your area. You are now taking interest into the upper class men students. People from other areas called you all the "OT's." The out of towners. They had different styles. Different langauges. You started liking the light-skinned girls in your gym class. Their was one particular female. She was a senior and you only seen her in gym class. She use to give you the attention but you knew she was on a different level than you were. She was older and doing things that you were just getting started with. Every day you seen her you had to say something. You made it your business to say something or did something that would catch her attention. At the same time their was another light-skinned female that you liked as well and lived not to far from you. She was active. You saw her all the time. All the guys wanted to get with her but she liked you out of all of them. You never understood why but you just went with the flow. Watching the other guys get mad because they did what all they could to get her but she was big on you. Every day you would hit on her. You made her blush a lot and she liked the attention that you gave her. She didn't have to try hard to get attention. She was popular. Very. You always thought she was on a higher level because all the guys that hit on her was the upper class men. It never worked because it was something about you that attracted her to you. She was on a higher level than you was. So you thought. She was already attracted to the cars and the money. Everything you didn't have, but you had what they didn't have and that was a sense of humor and the fact that you were social. You both was in the same grade but she was not in your same gym class in which the other girl was. You would have pool and knowing you could swim and dive, you could show off so she could see. See how you jump off the diving board in a swan dive. She had many classes with you and lunch time. She practicely invited you to her. She had game and you knew it. You liked it. She knew what you wanted and she played on it. She didn't live far so you would go see her and then she made it official. Boyfriend and Girlfriend. Other guys would just look. You calm down with the flirting thing and focused primarily on her. You didn't want her to know anything that use to go on within your home. So you play everything by ear. You like her. You would now walk the halls together. She was a female that you wanted to be with. She boosted your style and guys would look and the other female you started getting to know a different side of her. The quite side. The side she didn't show people and you also showed her she didn't see often in the other guys that she would attract. It was your intelligent side. She like the fact that you were different. That was the attraction at times she would show the physical side when you both are alone. When sitting down at her house you would be sitting between her legs and she would put her shirt over your head. One time she did it you turned around and she pull it back. Not because she was a tease, it was because she didn't want to move to fast, but she wanted to. She didn't want to interupt what yall was had going on as far as an early relationship. Days go on and she find out that one of her friends know you from back in middle school that you had a sexual encounter with. Funny how girls talk. Your feelings start to grow but she did not like the flirtatious things you did with other females. and in the end that was the breakup of you two relationship. You still have a strong feeling for her. You would later you will run into her again in the future once high school is over. 1997 was a good year. You always like to go to the store in building 10 because all females were there. It was the retail program. They worked the floor. You made sure you had money because as in you were in the carpentry class your teacher would take the whole class. You never took a lot because all you would but is the prezels that they sold that was only for a dollar. The walk was only 20 minutes with the stay going and coming back. You junior year was the same as the grades got promoted. Nothing ever changed at home. The fear of a terrible punishment and the yearn for attention from your mother starts to fade. School was out and as usual with your ability to read and write along with your comprehension skills you get promoted onto the next grade. The next level. 12th The summer was good and you get to explore more to the south with the family travel time to Georgia and North Carolina. This trips always been fun to you. It was time away from your city and friends and you get to experience different culture and meet different people from other states. Seeing how they live outside of where you live. The trips to Georgia was fun because you use to travel by train. They were long but comfortable. Your mother wanted you and your sister and brother to see different things other than what you saw in your neighborhood. Different ways of culture, styles, people, and language. More family times were cool and being spent than before. Your inner family financial state have improved. The home started looking more livable. More furniture with plants like spider plants and shade plants. Life was good as a young teen growing up in a poverty area. The ghetto is what people called it. September rolls around and back to school you go. This time around you were the upper class men. The seniors. The big dogs of the school. Your friend from 32nd street had a truck this time. Smoke out before and after. The regular.

The class work is easier and the shop class is easier as well because it is everything you have learned in the past 3 years you have attended school. It's a piece of cake. This time around you on your grown man statues. No longer a young boy and you carried yourself with class. Not to much running the streets and cruising the halls for all to see and for you to see all. Everybody has gotten older and now your class is the ones who run the school. Not as much school work is being done in your senior year. This year came girl trouble. You have now formed a relationship with a puerto rican female from around the way. She was quite, new, and beautiful. She wanted a boyfriend but her family had a different opinion about interracial relationships and being as those she was a female the mother was very strict. She had two brothers and another sister. By the time her mother found out she had a you was her boyfriend it was to late to end it. You really liked her as well as she did you. You would see her every day at school and you both rode the same bus. You enjoyed her company. She didn't know much about the streets and didn't hang on them at all. It was school and back in the house. This is one of the reasons you never knew she lived in your area. Whenever her mom would go shopping or to church, you would go over her house to spend time with her because she wasn't allowed to come out to play much. Whenever she did she would call you and you would show up wherever she was. You were cool with it because little did she know she calmed you down. One day which turned out to be a big learning experience in life to you was when she wanted you to be the first one to have sex with her. She was a virgin. You were already sexually active so you knew a little about sex. You were the teacher. When her mom went food shopping she called you up on the phone and gave you the okay to come to the house. In the basement was a basement that was left for her uncle that once lived with them. You didn't have a condom but decided to proceed without one. Huge mistake you have yet to find out. It was time you thought so you took it easy because it was her first time and you knew it would hurt her so to took caution. As you start, it hurted her so you took it slow. You never got to ejaculate because she wanted you to stop but later found out you didn't need to cum just to make a baby. Her mother come home and you were in the house. You stay in the basement as her mother and her sister helped bring in the groceries she had. AS you heard the footsteps on the floor go back and forth in and out of the house to the kitchen you plan your get away. The basement had a window that faced the front walk way. Once she got settled in the house and knew she wasn't going back outside, you decided it was time to jump up and climb out of the window and run all the way home. You were late being home but as long as you were there and not getting caught in her house you were cool. You thought about it all night and couldn't wait to see her in the morning. This morning was different the feeling you have for her as became deeper. You loved her and realize what falling in love with her. You was not the kiss and tell type of person. You were very private about your life. It was better knowing everybody is not in your business. A phone call on a Saturday morning came ringing in your house. Two weeks after you both did what you did. You were cleaning the basement with your family when the phone rang and her mother ordered you and you step-pops and mother to come to her house. Find you made nothing of it. When you got their you heard a shocking statement. Her daughter was pregnant. You sit in shock asking yourself how did that happen when you didn't even cum inside of her. Well come to find out when breaking a females virginity without a condom with the precum you can get her pregnant. OMG. How you ask yourself still. Her mother was upset. Even more upset because what happened in her house. The result was her caging up every opening in the outside of the hose. No way a person can get in or out without a key. Wow. You were happy and confused as well as she was but her mother was so upset the rope has gotten even tighter. Now as a senior with all that running around kissing girls in hallways now has a baby on the way. (sighs) Her mother automaticly thought being as though you were black you were not going to be there for her. Like what teachings have she been taught and who taught them. Crazy you thought. You were not taught this inside your home. It didn't matter what race you were their was good and bad in everyone. More prejiduce then racist. The damage is done and has no choice to have it because they are catholic so that means abortion is out. She felt a little easier in being pregnant because it did not change anything inside your relationship. You were happy and being a father was a big step up. She just inherited another family that is family orinetated. What you didn't know as well as your girlfriend of how her mother would treat you being as though she is now going to have a racially mixed grandchild. You call it the best of both worlds. Once you found out the child to be born was a boy, tears come your eyes. Happy at the fact that you may have a reflection of you that will carry your knowledge. A blessing. You would figure once you are there you will not jump ships. The respect for the mother will still be there. School was different from then on out. The bus rides are now different because now you are riding the bus with the one you called your latin queen. You having a boy flooded the school like a bad storm. In a good way though. There were talks going around the school with the girls because all the flirting you were doing in which you would stop because of a child you were expecting. There were times you would think of her mother and the fact that she is now going to be a grandmother and she will eventually love. She had the advantage and was not letting up. Her mother was cruel. You would get frustrated because even still that she is pregnant you were not allowed in her home nor was she allowed at yours. It's getting ugly and her mother is making it hard for the both of you. Mind you that your parents were church going people and the rules were still the same as far as staying out late. You could not do. Your parents were working people and was respected in your neighborhood. A great family that taught morals and respect. That was a must in all black families as you grew up. Their were no cursed words said in front of adults nor cigarettes being lit. Her mother was very pushy and vow to not stop her ways in her daughters in boys regardless of the fact that she was pregnant. You started taking liking to another latin female. You figure that if her mother would see that you were different she would change. It did not. Now you two are being watched closely by her older brother while you both rode the bus. On her mothers orders was to watch your every move and if he seen something out of the ordinary he was to report back to his mother which made it hard on her. You started looking for that attention in other places. As I said another female you started taking liking to. You and your new baby mom started having arguements because you wanted to spend time with her and in school wasn't enough. She was in the grade lower than you so you didn't see her all the time in the halls at school. She took a different program. She took CNA courses. You decided you couldn't keep the relationship going because the attention that you wanted she could not give you because her mother was in the way. She came around to your hose once or twice but was accompanied by her brother. Ackward situation but it was cool because they would come to your block were everything was going on at. All things she also couldn't do because of the strictness her mother had on you. When she would come it was cool. You both liked it because your parents dealt with it in a different manner. It didn't matter if the child was not all black. It was a child being brought into the world is all enough respect for them. She also liked coming because your parents did not treat her any different. She was apart of the family now. So it is what it is. You felt like crap when you did not see her. At the same token their was this female that always made it her way to come to your corner store every day. When she brought things she would not go straight home. She would stop past and see you. You were either outside playing street football or you would be just chilling with your friends. You decided to call it off with you and your baby mom. It was too dramatic every time you wanted attention and couldn't get it. She wanted to give you want you wanted because she wanted it as well but due to the divider that the mother had, you step away. Saying to yourself you would be there for her regardless so you started messing with the other girl. Didn't give it no rest time in between or nothing. You decided on day to take a trip to the waterfront with your new girlfriend. It was called "lovers lane." She came to your house to get picked up and you both decided to walk to there. You walked up the same street your baby mom lived on but was shy a block away until you seen here and her sister sitting outside in the step enjoying the nice weather. You stop and thought quickly. For her to keep walking and you would meet her a few blocks up past your baby mom house but what you didn't know is that her sister seen you. A whole block away. Chicks. (sigh) She continued on walking as you took a squat on the step next to your baby mom. Please like that would have worked. She was very upset and the sister was to. The question was how are you going to break up with her sister one day and start dating another female the next. Complicated you tried to explain but it did not work. You continue on and met up with the new girlfriend as you enjoyed the day all to yourselves. This is what you wanted from your baby mom but could not get because of the situation. Your second mistake was that they both rode the same bus. Everybody. The sister vow to fight your new girlfriend. As the days go on it was tension. You would go to the back of the bus and wait for the bus driver to pick up your girlfriend that would come back and sit with you as your pregnant ex-girlfriend would sit in the front with her sister and brother. You thought about how it made your ex-girlfriend feel all the time but once your new girlfriend come and sit with you all thoughts would go out the window but not the feeling. It went on for just a few days until one day as normal the bus would stop and pick up the friend and her cousin first then your ex, sister, and brother than soon get you. The next stop would be to pick up your girlfriend but this time was different. Once the school bus stopped and opened up the doors for the other students as usual, she steps on the bus but came to a pit stop with furies of blows coming from her sister. She started rocking her a after another and didn't stop until she fell out of the bus. Revenge was final. The word what happened spread like wild fire. Your baby mom was never the same after in entire incident She loved you and heartbroken at the same time. You can't help but to see her and to make sure she was good. That's all that you wanted for her to be okay. On one Saturday morning you were cleaning the basement with your family, the phone rang. You answer It was her best friend telling you to not get mas. She began to say that your baby mom had the baby. Shocked hurt and disappointed. She had your son and inspite of all that occured she did not have the aldacity to pick up the phone and call you and to say she was on her way to the hospital. You hang up the phone upset and had to tell your mom and step pops. Your step pops told you to calm down and he would drive you to the hospital. Your mom was just in shock that her grandson came, You arrive to the hospital excited that you are about to see your first born son. Once you get to the room you see her mom, cousin, brother, and sister. Everybody was their but you on some spiteful shit. Pardon my language. Very mad now but you did not allow that to overcome the entire reason what you were there. You ask where your son was. The response was down the hall. You go in a hurry to see your son. Beauty you seen for the first time from a new parent to his son. You say what's up little nigga in a slangful manner but what you did not see was her little cousin standing next to you. He was a kid. No more than five. He runs back and tell the family that you called your son a Nigger. You go back to the room with excitement. They were all upset over the comment that was taken of out content. A misunderstanding but that did not matter to you. You were happy. Forget all that happened in the past. Your son arrived. The next day you wake up with a different happiness. You wanted to see your son. Little man looks just like you. You go see your son in the hospital. It is now just you and your sons mother. You both have a good conversation and spoke about how she should not have taken away the fact that you wanted to see your son born. The results were you both was a new parent and still young. An understanding was made. You can see your son whenever. The birth certificate was signed in which she named your son. You had nothing to do with it. Still the revenge goes on. You go along with it. Not a good trip you can see already. School was back it and you wanted to tell the world. Pictures was shown and the new was everywhere. She has a new boyfriend and you are still with your girlfriend. She has the ball now and it is a game you will surely lose. Nothing matters at the time except the birth of your son. You go out and buy clothes and other accessories that is required for a new born She had all the big things like

Strollers baby car seat and many other things was brought with the baby shower that was thrown. It hurt hearing from her mother that the family don't need you. Her mother had a way of expressing her feelings about all of this. Taking away from you not seeing your son born was the last straw. You do not take the from a man that wants to see their child born. Rather it be a boy or a girl. One or two at a time. You just don't do that. You decisions were made better and every dollar that you had went to your son. She is now allowed to have a boyfriend in the house. Crazy how things turn but it had to happen to you fist. You can only blame yourself because if you would have just stuck it out with her things would have been different between you two. Now its time to spend with your son at your house without the mother. Father and son time. It should not matter who you show your son off to but it is to your baby mom. You went to your girlfriend house with your son. Some how some way your sons mother get a drift that you were there with your son. She came to your girlfriends house with your father demanding she get your son. At first you said no because you just got him for the night. It turned out to be a big thing outside of the girlfriends house. So big your girlfriend attempted to come after your sons mother to fight her. You turn and try to stop her while behind your back your sons mother is coming. You turn and push your sons mother back which only made things worst because of standing up for her you the mother of your son you stand up for your girlfriend. Your father get into the mix but when you tried to pump up at him you knew you could not beat him. You give her back your son and her and your father got in the car and left. Another devestating move. She says you can't see your son at all and she is taking you to court so you can get visitation rights. Bummer. Your son can be around her boyfriend but you can't take your son to your girlfriend house and now you have to go to court just to see your son and you did nothing wrong. The days went on without seeing your son. The day come and now you are in court. You were so happy to see your son that whatever the outcome was as long as you get to see your son. Visitations were arrainged and it was required that you see your son only if your mother was in the presents of you like you this big bad dude. You didn't like it but being with your son is all you wanted inspite of these supervised visitations. Being you and her were still under age her mother had full custody of him. It never works out for you because the grand mother still felt some type of way being as though you were black and it happened in her house. To bad. She was still acting like a bitch but loved the hell out of your son. She puts you on child support and she didn't even give you a chance to be there for your son. Spiteful bitch. You was providing more for your son than they were. Anything he wanted and needed he got and more. He had the world and didn't know it. Curse the evil. While all this was going on your step pops relationship did not get any better. You and your girlfriend break up and now the focus is on your son entirely. Your feelings for your sons mother never changed and the thought of getting back together always crossed your mind. When your son would get sick he would spend a day or two in the hospital for observation. New borns immune systems are not as strong to defend germs as if they were older. The immune system had to build up to fight of germs that sore the air. The communication between you and her was good but the tension was still their with the grand mother for no valid reason. Sucks to be you. You both agree that time will heal and the main focused is on your son and his health. You two one night were in the hospital together. You started looking at her with that look that she understood and one thing lead to another and you two were in the bathroom making out. One last time for the road. She loved you and you loved her back. Parenthood you thought. You graduated the following year and you wanted both her and your son to be there to celebrate your happiness. The partying would began with your school friends you probably wouldn't see again once school is completely over. You wanted to go out and party with them and their was a particuler female that was going to be there. Your sons mother could not go and wanted you to stay home with her and your son. You insisted that you both was not actually together and that she had a boyfriend. Even though you both did what you did inside the hospital bathroom was you two little secret. You went with your friends anyway. Little did she know that she was the mother of a soon to be street thug known in your area. At the end of the day it was her who got the heart break because you wanted to go out and party celebrating your graduation and you knew she was not allowed. Adding fuel to the fire. You could not go to the senior trip because of your behavior. You started thinking about what life have installed for you in the future. The summer is in and the partying just begun. No school the next year, what are you going to do. You seen your son when ever you had the chance to but it was either two things that was going to happen. Either you get a job or you had to get out. That was it coming from your step pops. You faked the over night job for awhile so you could hang out all night with your friends. That was soon to come to a halt. Home during the day and out during the night. You took a liking to a particular female at this time. Puerto Rican of course. This was your moto if its not a rican female you not dealing with them. Your preference of course. You can dance it now speak it a little and now you are deep in the culture. Yes you love the food. On one night you was walking on 10th st. With that female you took liking to. Your step pop was suppose to be at work but seen you walking. In your mind you said you would have to answer to him in the morning because you was suppose to be at work. In the morning he told you that you had to present a pay stub to him or you had to get out. So what you think happened happened. It came to that Thursday where you had to present the pay stub. You knew you didn't have it so you already planned to leave once he said get out. You packed your clothes and headed outside to the real world. You moved over philly with a female friend that had her own 3 bedroom house with two young sons. You took the back room and they had the middle. Most of your friends were females. You didn't trust the guys that much. They dealt with ego issuses all the time. With hanging with them you gained popularity. They were older than you so you seen a lot of things. Everybody thought you were having sex with them but you were not. That's how you gained the trust inside their click is what you called them. All of them were older than you was and they liked the fact that you were around because your opinion mattered. From a male perspective. You seen them in linguria. Asking for your opinion in which you liked because you got to see what woman liked that pleased the guys and you got to see their bodies. OMG. You kept your cool all the time and that kept you around. Getting noticed by the older guys who were driving bikes and big cars. Loud music and all. You loved the lifestyle. Latin Quarters was the famous club in North Philly. The Bad Lands is what they called North Philly and you were there. Seeing all the big dope deals. Cars on rims. Loud music coming from the systems that played in the cars. This is what you seen as a kid growing up and now you are out there with it. You had no job but you found your way every night to get high and drunk. This was the life so you thought. You went to parties and the females wanted you around because when a guy approach them that they did not find attractive they would say they were with you so the guys would back off. It worked every time. You loved it because you were at all the parties, drinking, smoking weed you was the man. Without money. You got your first tattoo in Philly. You were attending the Puerto Rican parades in Camden and in Philly. All was good until your friends boyfriend come home from prison and tells her that he wants you to get out. Bumper. Not only are you having fun and enjoying the summer but you do not have another place to go. He thought you two were having sex and it wasn't even like that. As I said male egos but you understand from a male aspect of things. You were around mommies all the time and had access to all but never touched and for him to think that was crazy as you seen. No time spent with your son and now have to find another place to stay. Wow. You not mad at her but upset of how the situation went down. You now walking all the way down Alleyegany with a big trash big full of clothes on a hot day of the summer. You called your friend from high school which is a female and her older sister was one of the ones in the click you hung with. You explain the situation and once again it was the Puerto Ricans who let you in. Crazy but they were your friends and you knew if worst come to worst they would not see you on the street. The older sister was the life of the party. All the guys wanted to get with her. Loyalty is what you knew. Now living with them was a little different but was the same. At night you all partied. Smoked weed and drank. Still keeping it going. You had no girlfriend at the time and hung with your friend Ruben. Ruben was younger than you but he was rican so he automaticly fit in. His mom didn't care to much on what he did because she knew he was raised right so he wouldn't get into trouble. He liked the fact that you hung out with all the girls so you both relationship as friends became close and cool. One day you both got approached by a street hustler. He was older than you two and wanted to see if you both wanted to make money. Once again another opportunity to make money but this time your mom, step pops, father, or step mother wasn't around. He said he been looking at you two and wanted to know if you both wanted to make money. This time when you got introduced to the game it was different. The dope game. Money was different so was the customers. Officially a dope boy and got the best training from the block from the OG's to it. You and Ruben was each others look outs while the other hustled. You couldn't bring drugs into the house you were staying in because the respect for them you had more than the streets. The loyalty you had for your friends was more than the street drugs and people. You moved out and moved into your grandmothers house that was right up the street from the block. Perfect you thought. Full time block boy. That was your job. It put money in your pockets so you respect the game. Respected the rules. Moving in with your grandmother was cool. She was the brickhouse and you were smart. She understood your situation and as her grandson she didn't want to see you on the street. She would rather have you in her care than anybody else. She worked doubles all the time doing CNA work. She loved to take car of the older people. You had the front room and you could see the block from your room. You were making money. Now you are 18 with a lot of money helping out with the rent and expenses You kept the same crew with you and Rubun. You then got control over the whole block. Now you are 18 and you have a lot of money. You are helping out with the rent. You went from case working both shifts, from moving to night. The guys that owned the block with in with the Sons of Malcolm X. They liked the way you ran the block and you your family was in. They liked the way you moved and knew they could trust you. You was a breed of soilders and now excerice the ability. You played it well. You grow from a h\small time hustler to the youngest on the block to have the most money. You never flashed money and did not wear jewlery. Just stacked. The people that owned the block paid you 1,000 every Friday off the top. The first ten bundles you sold was yours and so on. At the end of the night you treated your workers to beer and liquor they had there own money for their own way. That's how you kept your circle. You still hung with the girls and they started to hear you was the man of the block and you were their friend. They thew parties and you supplied the lour and paid for the dj if needed. Party on anyway. You are now the life of the party. A little big boy. You was the one who never like attention, never drew heat and moved accordonely because you knew that where to was living at involved your grand mother. You now get introduced to guns. Your first gun was a 380 glock. pretty and it came with a holster. Just given to you. One night you heard the police was coming so you ran to the block behind you and blended in with crowd and that's when you met Angie. They never knew what you di but they knew you were from up the street. Really didn't know what you did but they went with it. You asked Angie for a drink of her beer. She said yes. You drank her whole bottle of a 40 once. She was upset a you vow to pay her back. The police never came and you went back to the block. You didn't have to be there. You just made sure the night was good. Like an extra eye. The owners liked the fact that you lived a block away and you watched all things. Every night was the same. At the end of the night you made sure everything was good. All was accounted for. Everything was put up and it was time to go to the liquor store but this time was different. The girl that you drank her bottle wanted you to buy her another bottle. A 40 once. Okay you gave the workers money to buy liquor and you and her would go your own route. While walking to the store you seen your uncle in which she knew him to. He said go ahead with your bad self and do your thing. You and her went to the liquor store to buy the 40 once and pint of Hennessey and you took her to your room where you both drank and played music. She did not know you were the man of the block but you enjoyed the night with her. You both rocked out all night long. You woke up the next morning and handed out what needed to open up the block. She was still sleep while you did what you had to do. You told her to go get a set of clothes to bring them back so she could take a shower. Once she came back she came with her older sister. She showed her the scratches she made on your back from the night before. Her older sister knew who you were dealing with and she put her up on her game. If she wanted to keep you knew what she had to do and prepared her for what she was to incounter in dealing with you if you was to keep her around. She knew who owned the block and her approvel was good. Once she got her self together you told her you was going to take her shopping. You and her went to the Galary over Philly. You told her she can get what ever she wanted. You both came back in a cab with a trunk full of clothes that you had brought for her and told her she can never go back to where she was. She was your girlfriend and she could have whatever she want. Every girls dream. Shopped til she dropped. The day was good and the fellas made money. It ended with her as your girlfriend and she loved it. The next day you took her shopping again. 2 day shopping spree. She had all what all girls wanted. Jewlery, winter coats, sneaker, earrings the works. Bath and Body lotions. Hair sprays. Everything. She got hip to the game real fast. You were the dope boy. The man of the block and she was the queen and she knew it. The new bonie and clyde. Unsepreatable You knew she never had a guy that would just spoil her to death and to the grave she vowed. It came to a point to where your best friend at the time which was a female was upset saying how you just met her and took her on this 2 day shopping spree and didn't take her. She was your friend and understood but still was upset at the fact that you just met her and she got everything. Nothing changed with your friendship but she just made it known who she was to your girlfriend. Your sister even heard about it and it was her up and coming birthday. You made your sister happy on her birthday. You sent her home in a cab with a pocket full of money and drunk as hell. You now had it where things was going smoothly. The week went on as it should and at the end of the week you decided to go to your mothers house and take $1,000. Your mother looked at you and shook her head and did not take the money. You tried to give it to her but she would not take it. The next week you went to her and did it again. This time you dropped the money and walked away. You knew if you walked away she had no choice but to take it. It was times you would go to the local chineses store and see your son with his aunt and put $100 bills in both his pockets. You still did for your son when ever you seen him. You was to busy running the block, you didn't have time to see your son but knew he was good. You still read books and brought them. Knowledge was the key to all things and that you knew. You were quite humble and smart. The streets were raising you now. Your sisters birthday was coming and you know you had to make it worth wild. A birthday she was trying not to remember. You got her. You was her older brother. People Knew you but didn't know what you really was doing. You moved swiftly. Your new girlfriend was good and everybody who knew here knew she had it. She walked with a different walk. Her friends was cool with the fact that you was her man because she had the money to do what ever she wanted to do so when ever she wanted something to drink it was like how much they want. You did not need a car because you was always on foot. If you had to go anywhere you could just call a cab a be out. Life was good so you thought. You wore nothing but Eddie Baurer and she wore Old Navy. New Years would come around and it would be memorable. You took care of those who was with your crew and around Christmas you took care of those who was less fortunate. You thought you was untouchable and you had the ride or die chick. Wifey is what you called her. You got a tattoo with her name and she got yours. You now become obsessed with tattoos. You was getting them like every 3-4 days. You seek knowledge as a youngster and have bumped into the older guys that are on the block with you. They had the knowledge of self. God bodies. 5%ers. Mathematics and the Alphabets. You were sharp. You even surprised them with the knowledge. You already had book knowledge but was fooled by the tricknowledge that have been feed to you for years. You were sharp. You even surprised them with the knowledge you had. You already had knowledge because of all the books you read but was brain washed by the media. One day you were standing on the corner with your girlfriend and a car pull up and was trying get with her. She told them to back off as you watched her getting with them. You didn't say anything you just watched her. You just studied the situation. She handled the situation well. Knowing you had a team that would kill if something wrong happened. She finally said that she had a man and that you was standing right there and knowing you were the man of the block who ran the dope. You finally said something and if they wanted to fight lets get it on. They just got in their car and said they will be back. You waited for them to come back. You sat on the block at least for 20 minutes and decided that they was not coming back and you wanted to smoke some weed so you and her went home. Once you got their your got some weed out and rolled it in a philly blunt. A knock came to the door and you opened up the bedroom window and was announced that they did come back and you wasn't out their and they stuck up your boy Ruben for his jacket. You took that as disrespect and went to grab the gun you had. Your girlfriend told you not to go outside of the house with it. You told her you were coming back and for her to be in the house once you get back. Ruben, and one guy that was out there when it happened jumped in a car a drove to where there hung out at. You was in the back seat as they approached the guys on their corner where they was. Your friend who was the driver got out and demanded for the jacket back. He said no and you rolled down the window and started firing shot at everybody. All you heard was the gun firing and windows breaking while everybody ran for cover. You friend pulls off fast and everything was cool until a cop pulls up behind the car. He follows yall for at least 15 minutes before cutting on his lights. The driver pulls over and waited. He was revving up the engine to the car. It was stick shift. You was telling him if he pulls off before the cop come to the window you was to give him directions to where to turn if he took off. Before the cop come up to the window he takes off. Why did he do that. He should waited at least until he got to the window before pulling off. He did not follow any of your directions and took his own path. While he was driving taking the police on a high speed chase, you told him once he hit a right turn for him to throw the gun out of the window. You handed him the gun to do so. He hit a couple of lefts and rights then he couldn't make a left turn he hit a pole. Everybody jump out and now its foot chase. You figure if everybody go their seprete ways they can't catch yall all. You ran at least two blocks before getting caught. The holster to the gun you had on you but you figure if they didn't find the gun you was cool. They took you to the station and you find out all of yall got caught and they found the gun. The gun was never thrown and it was found under the drivers peddle. One police came in with a tape recording statement that who you thought was your boy told on you. Rubins mom came to get him because he was under age and you and your so called friend went to jail. The police charged you with possession of a illegally concealed weapon. Your first charge ever. Your girlfriend posted your bail and you wee out in 8 hours. Discharged. Happy because you had the right female by your side. Once you got out of the county jail you walk straight to the block. She had it running as it should have been She held it down for you and posted a $10,000 bail with 10% which came out to $1,000. You had that all day. Proud of your Boonie. The block already sold fifthteen bundles of dope and its only 8:00 in the morning. Lets get it. In North Jersey they call it 3 bricks. You told the big boys what happened and they would take car of it. You knew what would have happened if you told them how it went down. They wasn't to be played with and everybody knew it. Come to find out the guys that you was shooting at were all apart of the same family. You all met and the beef was squashed immediately. You now finding out that that big boys was big boys of a few blocks. Now you are seeing the bigger guys like "JR" who ran the "Alleyway." You met guys like Chill Will, Cito in which you already knew because your aunt has a son by his brother. You learned how to mix dope and expand it and bag it up. You are now deep into the game. You now owned a shotgun and a .22 caliber rifle. You seen so much money and now you don't plan on leaving the block. You also had the most loyal chick by your side. Things started getting heavy and you took on your girlfriends house as an additional stash house. You did not want to continuously put everything in your grand mothers house. You gave her friend a shirleen jacket with a pair of swirl earrings as a down payment for keeping things at her house. You bought her her own pager so you can keep in contact with her in case you needed her. Your girlfriend already had her pair of earrings and jacket. She was the first to walk the streets with a shirleen jacket, swirl earrings, and Timberlen boots. Now Cito use to come back from Philly to see the king pin named "JR." You knew that JR had a million dollar flow in the Alleyway but Cito flow was even bigger over Philly. JR owned Cito and disclosed amount of money. Cito was getting upset over the fact that he had to keep coming to Camden to approach JR about it and JR was tired of him coming to him about it. Everybody who knew JR knew that he had shooters and he wasn't nothing to play with. Everybody who knew Cito knew he wasn't nothing to be fooled with neither. Both was feared and loved by many. On one particular night Cito came to confront JR about the money owned to him. As you knew JR was not the one to approaching about any situation let alone money. The result was Cito not getting anything and as he attempted to leave the whole situation by going back over Philly, he never made it. He was approached by a guy riding a bike at the red light. The guy opened fired and Cito was shot dead inside of his vehicle. That night devastated the entire city. All that knew him knew that we lost a good soilder in the streets of corruption and gun violence. Tradgedy. The hood goes into mourning. A memorium is still hung to this day in the memory of a good guy. R.I.P Cito. Unsolved murders was everywhere and with a new mayor running for office things was about to change. Mayor Milton Milon. Everybody who was from the streets knew that JR was aiding the campaign for the up and coming mayor. The king of the city wanted it in the palms of his hands. He paid local drug users to go out and vote come election time for Milon and they would use that very same money they were being paid for to buy drugs from the organization that JR ran. JR never really lost money. He dished it out for a reason and got it back through purchases from the people who he gave to money to. It was a win win for him and he loved it. At election time the new mayor of Camden was Milton Milon. JR now owns the city. Well his part of the city along with others. Mayor Milton Milon was in office for at least 2 years until he came up with this police force the would battle the streets on drugs. The war on drugs was apart of his campaign. In the month of January the block that he grew up on got raided. That was the block you case worked. 5th & Grant. They hit you guys hard. It was on a regular morning. When you thought nothing would happen. You was in one of the houses on the block It was a house that got turned into and apartment. One of your friends stayed upstairs and the apartment on the bottom was unlocked with a queen size bed mattress and box spring in the bedroom and nothing else in the house. It was not a hang out. You did not want to get both apartment raided because of the unneccessary movement in and out of the apartments. So on this particular day you was in the bottom apartment eating a chicken cheese steak that you had brought from a local famous food eating spot called "Ruthies." Their was one of your friends from the block eating his food as well. You heard one of guy from the block run through the front door and leaned up against it. You heard a loud kick then your friend that was there jumped up and ran to the back door. You just sat there. You did not have anything on you. No money or anything. The door wines up getting kicked in and the guy that was behind the door fell to the floor. The police come in with mask on and guns drawn. They tell you to get up and put handcuffs on you and excorted you out on the front porch. They caught your friend that ran to the back in the yard. He also sat on the porch with you. He had something in his pocket. Thats the reason why he ran but never got away. Three guys came to you. Two of them had guns but the other did not. He just looked at you then walked away. The other 2 left with him. They got into a truck that was parked on the side of the house. In your mind that had to been the mayor with his bodyguard. The raiding police took a photo of you then let you go. They did not catch you doing anything or any money in your pockets. They locked up whoever was standing on the corner and they stayed on the corner all day betraying to be hustlers. They would sell them whatever they wanted then lock them up a block away. They incarserated over 200 people that day. Mostly the drug users. The police stayed out there until 12 o'clock at night. Locking down the entire block. Milon has his publicity and you lost money. The owners of the team you was on was upset but he knows this come with game you are in and playing. They had money from the other raids they have conducted. The next day you attempted to open up the block with something new but the police had the block shut down so bad that not that many people came out. It went from $2000 to $1000 to $200. You had money so you had to stick it out and rebuilding at the same time. You and your boonie had a big aurguement and you needed space to get things back in order. She did not understand and thought it was another female. That was surely not the case. As easy as the money came you spent as well. Even though you had money, you couldn't accept the fact that it is not money coming in like it use to. With that new task force and their knowledge for the streets, blocks began to fall. You began to think that all they are doing is shifting the drugs movement down in one part of the city, the money will go to a different part of the city. The Alleyway. You presents was still needed so you stayed loyal tot he block. As you stayed all of your attentions was on the block, your girlfriend started to annoy you. Costantly in your ear you asked her to go stay with her family for a little bite, she thought you was having another female coming over. She decided on one night to take the fire exsinsher from the house across the street and decided to smash the side of your twin cam that you was preparing to be in the puerto rican parade. Once you came out she ran into the house and didn't come out. You waited until here brother came around the corner. You explained that she tried to smash out your car window and he couldn't get mad at you. He had to surppress her anger and had to show and prove to her that no female was in the house as she assumed. It got even worst, come to find out the house that you had bundles at was short on bundles. Somebody had been taking some and you had to pay for it. You didn't have all the money so you gave up your baby to cover the debt. You gave up your car. It hurted so much when they towed her was. Nothing changed with you and her relationship and you decided to move on to another block to hustle on to get money back in your pockets. You were wasting it spending money on her and maintaining your lifestyle. You forgave her and let her back in on the condition she was to find a place and you will give her the security deposit and some spending money until she gets on her feet. She agreed and it was time to not have relationships with no one but you will play in the sand box a little with females. You met another female and your ex came back around. You swung an episode with your ex but your main focus was on the new friend. You was on the block and the shift was over. You was texting the new friend while hustling. On the way to the spot where she is suppose to come pick you your ex pop up out of no way. You tried to lesson to what she had to say while you are walking, the car pulls up. You quickly introduse the two still walking you jump in the car and you and the new friend take off. Angie was mad at the fact that you are moving on and you do have the money to wine and dine another female. You didn't want to spend money on this new friend but I you wanted to see where it would go and if it was to go further it is what it is. The next day you went to your normal spot and once you got there your friend was there. It was cold outside so you gave her your jacket. Angie noticed that she had your jacket and was mad at the fact that she never wore your jacket. A fight was about to happen. Angie went to snatch the jacket off of the new friend. The girl defended herself and retrained. Punches started to ge thrown and on thing lead to another. The fight landed on your best friends mom car and the windsheild wiper got broken. The new friends brother was across the street with his crew and their girlfriends, He came from cross the street to gab her and they went back to their party. The friend still had the jacket. A court date came in the mail. Your possession of a undisclosed handgun. You went to the court appearance and you didn't have a lawyer. You bumped into your cousin and he had a lawyer on deck. You used his. You had money so you went with him. You went to see him at his office and then you was to discuss the payment arraigment with him and the case. You make the initial payment and a couple others and in the end the result was you getting five years probation. It was your very first lesson and the advice was, slow down. Now the days go on. Angie decided to walk down the street with another dude just to upset you. She knew what she was doing because when she walked passed she looked at you and looked away. The guy did not know what was going on. To him he was just walking through. You gave her that look like if you walk through here again she mess around and dude hurt and she didn't. You and Angie wine up getting back together and the hustle game was back on but on a different block. You was going hand and hand from 3-11 shift. Just like a regular job. It's funny how the hustle game and schedule is the exact replica of a legal gig. Shifts, managers, workers, and all. It's like you get paid off commition. It was the same block Angie lived on with her grand mother and aunt. She is outside with you but not on the corner. She mainly stayed at home or doing what she does with her friends. The fact that you are on probation did not matter. You claimed you knew what you were doing. You walked right into probation seen a whole lot of people and just walked right out. Bench warrant. You hustled day in and day out. You eventually took over both shifts. Just like you did when you was on 5th & grant. This time you are on 6th & bailey. You knew the owner of the block and he liked the way you made money. You hustled hard. Everyday. Everything accounted for. No shorts. You made friends in the drug world. At the end of every night was the same thing, drugs and alcohol. You started to smoke PCP (wet). Everybody was smoking it. You would go over Philly in the bad lands to buy it. Sometimes when you went over there you would see people you haven't seen in a while because they was on the run from the law and doing their thing over there. Drug game mean. That was the thing then. Wet, weed, and alcohol. Everyday. You and Angie was once again Boonie and Clyde. You bought guns and Angie was right along side of you smoking and drinking too. Back to that lifestyle. At the end of everyday the sex was good. You hustled so much that you barely slept. The day would come to where all would end and you knew it but still hustled. The big guy loved it. Everyday was like a chase. You chased the money everyday and had a look out for the police because you knew you had an open warrant for your arrest so you moved how you moved. Just had to stay out the way of the bounty hunters. They never seen your face until one day you was making a transaction. You did not have any lookout and thought you just to smooth to get caught. Untouchable you began to think again. The police pull up on you while in the mist of a traction. You look up and everybody ran. You ran right into them. They already had you pinned, you just didn't know it until you came out of the other end of the alleyway and they were right there. Game over. Possession of CDS and a violation of probation. First time you in the county jail more than 24 hours and can't get out because of the VOP. NO BAIL! 19 years old and you don't know a thing about jail except the stories that you hear from the people that have been in there. Untouchable no more. Now you are a inmate with a number. You quickly adapt. You know people and they know you. Your grand mother did not tell Angie to leave. All in all she is your closet friend and she was fly with your grand mother. You were into the nation of Gods and Earths so you quickly took to the ones that were. Time to keep your head into the books. You took the time out to actually learn the lesson of the nation and read everything that came through the doors or by your cell and in others. You were already humble and all for as munch knowledge as your brain could take. Knowledge, wisdom, and understanding can lead out of the stages of the dumb, deaf, and blind. At this era the nation and Gods and Earths was at a all time high because the style that came out of New York was the wave. Teaching you that you as a black man with the origin came from the the beginning are Gods and he controls his actions and them around him. By giving you principles that you can apply upon your life and actual facts dealing with the world as a whole can make you smarter than others because you would now possession the knowledge of self it enhances your as decisions as obstacales in life come at you once your get released from prison or jail was the storm is over. You were sharp with your words and with knowledge from reading books already you were mentally challenging. You attempted to fight your case but all in all you were caught red handed so you wine up going to a correctional facility for the first time as well. While you were in the county you met the bother of the ex girlfriend that you was messing with out Cramer Hill that you were going to have sex with but was interupted by bad company that nearly ended in a street brawl with you getting your ass kicked. You both talk things out and said it was immature but understandable. The days go on and you took heed to a older guy that was very known inside the jail by the c/o's and had loads of knowledge. You listened to him a lot. He had a reputation of starting movements in side jails and prisons. A threat to the DOC. The tier seen his work one morning at breakfast. He ate at a particular table and at this time their was a guy in his spot. This guy had weight on him. He worked out but so did the very knowledgeable man. The guy might have gave him a little shove and all hell broke loose. A fight broke out immideditely. Blood everywhere. Shocked everybody. Respect had to be shown. The fight was broken up by the time the c/o's found out that a commotion was going on. The tier was on eggshells all day but it eventually calm down as the days go on. You wine up getting a court date only to sign up for a public defender and to go back to your tier. Sucks. The proccess behind court appearances you will soon find out. As time laps before you go back to court you keep your eyes in the books and played chess. Met new people and started to learn about the law library. Months go past and you finally get another court date. This time was to enter a guilty or not guilty plea you would enter. NOT GUILTY you pleaded. Time to go back and sit until they indict your charges. You go back after seven months and decided to plea guilty because you was caught red handed. Time to go down for the first time. Your mother upset at you and did not accept any of your collect calls. Nervous but it was your doings that got you there no one elses. Time for brown bags call That's what they called it when your name was picked to get shipped out to what is known as CRAF. A facility you go to get classified to any prison in New Jersey they people see fit. You go through what is called cornteen. You had to be stripped naked, yelled at, humiliated, showered, photoed, and placed in your cell with another person you did not know awaiting to go to see the doctor to take blood work and a entire physical top to bottom. A few days past where you then have to see classification. You get classified to Garden State Youth Correctional Facility. You didn't know they called it "Yardville." You here stories about it once you get back to your wing. The day goes on with your mind in curiousity mode. You work out hard now because the facility had free weights and dumb bells. You are social so you speck with the guys in the big yard. You get cool with a few. Mainly out of towners because they moved different. You chilled with people from your area but you was still observing things because you have never been this far into incarseration. It is the morning your name gets called to be packed up and shipped to the ville. You took everything. Your underwear was to small so you had a problem at that. Your status is full minimum. You in there. You get stripped again then get chained from hands to ankles so you can't run or grab anything. You now take the ride to your distination arriving at what it looks from the outside a collage. You get excorted into the facility by c/o's. Once inside it start to change a little. You see a little bit of bars but more plaques and awards on the walls. You name is called and the question which is asked of you is to resight you SBI#. In which you do because you have to remember it for your entire stay. In and on the way out. You are now told where you and the other inmates had to go. R-house. One man cell on a tier with 15 rooms on both sides and 2 showers with one T.V. and a pool table with the phones on the wall so you can place a collect call with he pin number that they gave you. You now have to sit and wait until you see classification where they now place you according to your status. At this time you can smoke inside the building and they sold cigarettes on canteen. A guy approached you and asked you if you would like to trade a pair of your under clothes for something to smoke with matches. You did ASAP. Now you are a little more relaxed because you can just sit in your room with new ports and the lessons to resight. It was the summer time and your room is hot. No air conditioners. It is even hard to sleep at night. Your window stay open all day but no breeze at all. You finally see classification and they tell you with your status you go the the MSU. (minimum units for the inmates who have full minimum) The next day you go to the camps. Outside all day. Extra food. Free weights with dumbells. Only 10 other guyes on the wing. Single bunk. You even see some friends from your hood you haven't seen in awhile. He been down so long he even have a CD player with CDs. You straight. He was the biggest in the unit you were on along with one other guy. You can tell all they did was workout together. Now its time to socialize. Learn the ropes and who next in the weight room. You job is to go to school for mechnics. You were picking up weight. They was giving out loafs of bread and drank milk that was in a bag. Straight from the farms. Milk extra thick. You mom sent you some money and you began to order ensure on canteen. You hit the weight room right after dinner with another guy from Plainfield. You get into more books that they had down there already and hooked up with he guy that had knowledge of self. The days are coming to where you have to parole to see if they are going to let you out on parole. They mail you a paper that have to provide an address to where you want to be paroled at. You use your so-called girlfriend Angies address because its taking your mom awhile to respond to you asking her can you use her address. While locked up your mom moves out Sicklerville. She and your step pops along with your sister and brother now reside. Its time to see parole. You never seen them and they never seen you. That is a good thing. They ask you questions about your crime in which you admit to and they ask you a series of questions. They ask you to go sit outside of the room while they make a decission. You get called back in and the decission was to release you in December when you have a full year in. Yes! You go back to your unit excited. Now you go hard in the weight room. On the count down to freedom your ex-girlfriend sends you a surprise letter. This is the girlfriend that got taken away from you once the mother found out that she is no longer a virgin. She sends you a photo of a daughter she has had. Wow. Surprise! Your so-called girlfriend did not write you since 2 months in your bid. She only allowed you to use her address because you was now trying to come home. The love has died because she did not hold you down while you were locked up. You and your ex is writing each other back to back letters. Long letters playing catch up. In this process your mother sends you a letter saying you can use the North Camden address but its to late. You would have to switch once you get out on the streets. Its time to go home on parole. You have your things all packed to go and you say your goodbys. You go through the process of leaving the correctional facility. They give you train tickets and you wait for the van to take all who was getting released to Trenton train station. It feels good to leave free and do what you want. You walk in to speak to some one about what train you need to board to go home. You wait for the train hop on and enjoy the ride all the way home to Camden. You get to Camden and got ahold of your mom in which she came to pick you up. She arrives and you give her a big hug and she break things down in the car how things have been going. You get to her new house which is big and greet your sister and brother with hugs as well. Pictures was taken and you ate. Feels good to be free. Now its time to see your friends before you go to your so-called girlfriends house. You are dropped off in North Camden and you are greeted with bottles to drink as a celebration of being free. You drank and arrived at your girlfriends house drunk. She and her mother is happy to see you. It is night time so it is time to relax. You pass out and pissed on yourself as you were sleep. Man what a night. Your intentions is to move your things that she have bought you to your mothers house and tell your new parole officer that you were making the move so she can approve of it. She does and now its time to move your things. As you are home you are seeing your ex and tells her you live at your moms house on 9th street so she don't know about your so-called girlfriend. You was byeing time to tell your girlfriend that it was over and to not get caught with your and moving without your girlfriend knowing until the job is done. You tell her that you are moving to your moms house and she does not want no one to be in there with you but you. She don't understand why and is upset at the fact that you were moving. One day you are at your new home and your girlfriend is in there with you and a knock is at the door. It is your ex wondering why she haven't seen you in a couple of days and just making sure you were ok. You come out the door and leave it cracked while you tslk to her. Angie was standing on the stairs and knew it was a female you were talking to but couldn't see who she was. The night came and you had your ex in the house and knock came at the door and it was your girlfriend. She pushes her way in and see your ex in the house. She is mad and she starts to fight with you going to the kitchen to grab a knife from the draw to d\stab you with. She gets a hold of one but you grab her wrist and have her pinned against the sink. The grab it from her and she hits you in the face. You pushes her to the front of the house so she can exit the house. She is kicking and punching you repeatedly. You ex sees how you are getting hit as you try to get her out and you not hitting her back she intervene. She jump between you to and now the fight is between them to. You open the door so you can grab a hold of your girlfriend to put her out. As you push her out the house your friend that lived across the street was coming up the stairs onto the porch. As he enters the porch the door flies open and your girlfriend come out the screen door yelling she going to call the cops. You friend looks in shock that all was going on and you tell him you will talk to him later and go back into the house. You jump on the phone to call the police to tell them what have happened and that if someone calls them in a matter of a fight happening they would know. They said they will send somebody out. Luckily you did do that because when they came to the house they had said that their boys were at your now exes house with a call saying that she got jumped. They take your statement and you tell them you are on parole and you just wanted to tell them what happened and that she did not get jumped. You all had to go down to the precient to but on file all that happens. Once down their all what happened from coming home from prison to that night is revealed in front of you ex-girlfriend. She is in the state of shock to hear all the was built up to the night. Yall all are released with court dates and it is time for you to tell your ex all what you did. She understands and just was upset at the fact that you did not tell her instead of her finding out the way she did. She still wants to mess with you but tit is time to split ways because it is late in the morning. The night ends and the next day come and you go to parole to let them know what happened. They did not both with it and just said take care of it. The days go on and she is now with you. You get a job but want more money. You was use to having money. You went back to your old block and they have a opening for you in the morning. You start in the mornings when you was not working. You back on you r grind and you haven't been out for a month. You making a couple of dollars along with the money from work. You save everything. One day you are on the block and you had to go see parole. You sell a couple of bundles and decide to leave then come back. On you way walking home you notice a cop was following you. He would ride past you then come the other direction. Like he was seeing here you was going. When he turns down block and get out of the view of you, you disappear into your peoples house to give them the money and tell them what you were ding. They asked you if you were coming back to the block after you see parole. You replied yes and that you were going to just keep 3 bundles so you can go back to the block once you leave from seeing them. You give them the money and you went along your way in which where you lived at was only 2 blocks away from them and that you were going to drop it off then go see parole. AS you exited the house you seen one of your female friends that you had it out for since high school. You stop to talk to her while she was in her car. As she was in her car you was bent over talking to her through her window and the same police rode past you looking at you. At the same time the your ex was walking up the street. The girl pulls off and you waited for your ex to walk up to you. You asked her if she wanted to come to parole with you if she wasn't doing anything. She agreed. You started walking and the same cop pulls up on you and decided to give you a pat down. Your ex kept walking. As the officer pate you down you knew you had the drugs on you. It was in you left side pocket. He patted you down the right side first as his left had were on your head. You stood their calmly. AS he switch hands to pat you down on you down on your left side, you took off running. It was ice and snow on the ground because it was the end of January. Winter time. As you are running, you into an intersetion and almost got hit by a car which slows down your running. The cop catches up and tackle you to the ground. He searches you and find the drugs you had your pocket. Back to jail you go. You ex was standing there upset. Back to jail again with a new charge. Wow you just got out of prison Violation with a new charge. Your old tactics of fighting charges kick in because you was curious in why the police did not stop you along time ago. They had plenty of opportunities. Your mother is so upset she will not even answer the phone for you. You know many people in there because jail it seems like all males go through living in an urban area that has less financial help by the mayor or governor. Your ex sticks by you and do the bid with you. She accepts all your collect calls and runs the phone bill up without her mom knowing. She visits you every chance she get. You have money on your books to order food and paper and stamps to write your ex and mother. Your mother is now going through her divorce and losing the house because she could not keep up with the moregage along with the bills by herself. So she move back to the house she owns in North Camden. More money for her because she owns her house but now she has to file banckrupcy. Months has past and you have picked up weight, have a job on the tier at night to clean, food for days, you are settled in for the long hall. You finally get your discovery and it says that they obsevered you and another person do a drug transaction. Not only once but twice. Your questions was if you sold to two guys where were they and why did they allow you to walk 4 blocks then decide to stop you along with you not having no money on you that would prove the illegal tansaction actually occured. Remember they never seen you go into your friend house to drop off the money. Clever but not to clever because you would have gave him the drugs too. You sat 15 months fighting it back and forth until they gave you time served with a guilty plea. You did it. Now you have to answer to parole in the violation. The entire time you were locked up that time counted towards the violation as well. You only had to do 16 months total on parole. With your job in jail work credits came off the back number and once the parole office did the calculations, you have maxed out your time in the county. Out of the blue on a Friday night your name was called to be released. You thought it was a game some one was playing. You guys do that from time to time. The other guys had to remind you that the c/o's called your name to leave. Off to the races. The food you had in your hand you just gave it away and packed your things so fast you forgot to grab your blanket. Back to the streets again. This time you are free as a bird. You go to your mothers house here you and every body there. Now what you going to do. Maxed out now its time to party. You get released on your girlfriends birthday and you planning on surprising her by showing up at her house unannounced. She doesn't know you have been released. You get freshened p to go see her. You go to her house and knock on the door. She answers behind the door and ask who is it? You say your name. All you heard was a loud bang. She fell on the floor. Excited at the fact that you are home. She opens with her hair half done. She was in the process of getting extencions put in her hair. She greets you with a big hug. You say hello to her mother which is real cool. She allows you to stay there with them until you both get your own spot. Its on. You felt funny living in her mothers house while doing the uchy cuchy. Crazy but it all works out. You eventually find a place and you both move into a house on the block you got locked up for. Your ex girlfriend Angie stays on the block to with her grand mother. Its crazy living with your girlfriend and your ex the one you all had a big fight in your house before you got locked up. Her aunt and uncle have a flow going with the weed along with a house flow on the same block. You decided to start a flow as well everybody has their own clientale but you are the younger one and you play the field. They all watch you take over. You came up with a proposal to combine with the aunt and you will do the bagging up and going hand to hand. You split everything right down the middle. Now you both are seeing money you got the flow going crazy. Everybody know the green house on Bailey st. Has that work and you elevate it with every purchase they get a free blunt. Only one. So now they really coming on late nights and all. You and your girlfriend smoke as well. Her catches on because she also smoke weed so she looking for the green house come to find out its yours. She doesn't say anything directly to you but indirectly she does. She dosen't have a problem with it because it is taking care of her daughters and grand daughter. She just want some for free from time to time. You cool with it because you like her mom she one of the coolest moms you could meet and she have a sense of humor. You tone it down a little bit because it is both of your house and you do not want to get it raided so from time to time you and the aunt would take turns. Keeps the cops guessing and can't pin point where it is actually coming from. You calm down and let the aunt retake the flow after you added more onto it. You couldn't take the constant flow. On the corner is your friends who have the dope flow going. You decide to jump in a little a day or two out of the week is cool with you. You can make enough money to pay what ever needs to be paid and what ever else. It is the summer time now and everythings good. One day you heard several gun shots. Loud and long. You didn't pay to much attention to it because people like busting off fireworks day and night.

It is like 7 o'clock in the evening. Cops are swarming and your boy who runs the block shut it down. You just thought it was because its to hot out with all the cop around. Moments later you find out that 2 of your friends that you know have gotten gun down with big guns. Two homicides and an attempt murder. Wow summer time huh?. A few days past and you hear two of your friends got nabbed for the murders and attempt. Crazy because on the day of the incident you seen the two who got charged around the same time they said it happened. Things happen when it gets hot out. The days go on and a fight kick off on the block between your friends girlfriend and another female. She says she is going to get her boyfriend to come down and show everybody whats up. We all waited for awhile. The night fall and three cars pull up and all females jump out. We all thought it was her boyfriend with his boys. Well well well what do we have here. A big fight break out with the girls and us. They started it. You can't come to a block with females expecting to fight guys. A bad outcome its going to be and it was. All the cars that pulled up got their car windows bricked and tires slashed. When we heard the cops everybody scattered like roaches when the lights get cut on. Everybody running for cover. Crazy night but most certainly not the last. One day you decide to sell some dope in the morning for a little bit then cool out the rest of sthe day. You made about $400 dollars in the matter of four hours. You decided to stop and told your girlfriend you was done for the day. Your friend came and asked you was you going to keep it going. Your response was no but you would case work the block for the remainer of the shift and still get paid for it. Your boy wanted to get the rest of the shift and you was cool with it. He turn in the money to you and you give him more work. Within a few hours he come to the house and say he thinks the cops are trying to get him. You say go in the house and go out the back door and for him to shut it all the way so it don't look like someone is back there or went through the back. He did. You stand on the porch and watch a cop ride past your house. You just sat their as you smoked a cigarette. Moments later you see that same cop come back around but this time he bring his partner. He comes up the one way. They parked across the street from you and ask you to come to them. You did because you didn't want them to look at you suspeciously. They did anyway. They were looking for your friend. They went into your house searching illegally. They came up with nothing. You are in the back seat of the cop car wondering why they told you to get into the car and you did nothing. The come out and wanted to give up the search until one of the officers said le him look one last time. He came out of your house with a brown paper bag that had 20 bundles of dope in it. He had a set of keys with him. He comes up to the car and ask you if they were yours. You say yes and in the back of your mind you were like if you don't say yes they will pin it on your girlfriend once she got back from her mom house. Once you said yes, they took you out of the car and cuffed you and gave you a distribution charge and a school zone. Back to the county you go. Damn you can not stay out of there. You in the county again and you thinking well as long as your boy got away you good. Just a thought because when you got processed and excorted to seven day you boy yell out the port hole in the cell door at you. You wondering how the hell he in there and made it there before you did. He tells you that they picked him up on third street buying weed. He didn't even make it home. Crazy. You didn't even get comfortable and they call your name to be released. Your bail was posted by your friend that ran the block. Real friend. You get released and found out that you have to go see the bail bondsmen to arrainge payments every week to stay out. You paid for the first 2 weeks and knew that with having no job you couldn't keep that up. You were already hot with a new charge so going back to the block was out. You called your cousin who needed help watching her kids while she works. You said you will watch them and she will pay you. This is the thing, she lived in Savannah, Georgia. Well here you come. You had to find out a way to tell your girlfriend and knew she would not like the fact that you were out of state but you had to go because once you missed a few payments to the bail bondsmen and that the bounties were going to come for you. You talked to your mom and decided it was best to leave a hideout for awhile until you can come up with a way to pay them every week. Didn't go that way. You go to Georgia without your girlfriend knowing. By the time they find out you wasn't paying you were already gone and they did not know where you was. You didn't know that if you didn't pay them they are going to attack the people who co-signed for you about there money. Your mom co-signed. Sucks to be you and you are now on the run. Savannah was nice. A new atmophere for you. You did not know how to cope but you adapt. Your cousin is planning on moving to another area. More open. Its nice. Four bedrooms and 1 1/2 bath. All on one floor. You now start to settle in. You start looking for the weed man and you find him. He lives in your complex and he is around your age. You later find out that you both had the same birthdays. You start cooling with him and look for an investment. Your cousin pays you for baby sitting and you take that to invest in weed with your friend. It flips fast. You both now jump up to selling powder as well. You find out that sniffing powder was a party drug in the south. Its cool to the younger crowd. To you being as though you from up North powder was a thing older people did not the people that were your age partying with it. You invest in that to. You on the run, living good and selling drugs. Back to your ways again but this time the police don't know you are a fugitive from New Jersey. You doing you. You now going to the club. Something you never did when you was in your hometown. Their clubs make you want to go to them every weekend. All the things you seen on t.v. Wow. The south is live like that. You fall in love with it. The woman are totally different. Just like the videos. Amazing. You don't want to go back home. The girls like you because you not from there. You have your run ins. But the clubs and the seen are is different. The air even taste different. The clouds look like somebody put cotton balls in the sky. From the trees to the grass. Man is this what the south is like. You fit right in. You kick it with every girl you seen. You get lashed to this one female that works in Applebees. A waitress. She is hip to things and she smokes weed. She introduce you to different types of wine. You drinking every night while you watch your little cousins by day. Its cool because they are your family so you help raise them as well. Your cousin is married and he is cool so the household is pleasent. You feel free for the first time. Every morning you would take a chair and sit in the front of your door to enjoy the fact that you are free for the first time but yet on the run. One night you and the girl from Applebees had a fight at your apartment. She punches you in the face while you are pushing her out the door. You grab her and slams her on the couch. You land on her leg in which she injurues. She limps to the car and you block her in as you call your cousin on the phone for her and her friends to leave the club so they can come there and beat her up. As she sits in her car she calls the cops. Your cousin pulls up and the girl did not want to get out of the car. The cops come and all of you are in the house. They all excited and the girl claiming to be in distress but she cool so she just want to go home. One of the girls who liked you seen a scar on your face and she tells you to go some alcohol rub to put on your face. You go grab it and put it on your face it aint bout bout nothing. The cop asks you for your name and walks off. He then comes back and tells you if you wanted to press charges and if you she was to press charges you both was going to jail. You said no and she said no. They left and she left as well. One of your cousins friend liked you. So from that day on you two where on each other but the thing was she was married. So it didn't get that close because she was married but it was boiling and fast. She was from New York so you both had the same swag. It reminded her of back home to her. Your cousin get galled to be deployed to Iraq. She was in the army. She gave you the keys to the truck and said you can drive it while she was away. Her husband had his own car so you were good. One day while she was gone you and the fellas decide to go to the strip club that sat at the border of Georgia and North Carolina. You all pack inside of the truck and roll out as Ludachris would say. Once you got there, it was females everywhere. One girl come up to you all indivisually. She asks everyone one by one if they wanted a dance. She got to you and asked you. You say no but your boy might want one. She goes to him and start dancing. After she was done, she came to you and asked you again. You say the same thing go ask your boy. She goes and dance with him again. After she is finished she comes to you and tell you that you have to pay her for the dances. You kindly tell her you did not tell her to go dance with them you told her to ask them instead and that you was not giving her a dime. She then goes to the bouncer and tell them you was not paying her for the dances. The bouncer says that you have to leave and your boys have to go with you. You just laugh it off and say thats the fasted you ever got kicked out of somewhere. Your boys not even mad. You roll up some weed and you all jump in the car and ride back home while you all smoke weed enjoying the night. You saved money so you don't care. The night ends well. Days past and you get a phone call early in the morning saying you need to come out the house and go through the back and climb through a window that was going to be open for you. You and your boy are curious to why you got a call like that but you go along with it. Your boy finished rolling up a blunt with weed then leave the house. Once you exit the house you notice that two bounties were coming in your direction. They were looking at you and told you to not run. You had your two nephews with you and could not actually run and leave them even though they were with your boy. They are your responsibilities and you just gave up. You put your hands on top of your head and took a squat in the dirt. Times up. (sigh) Thy hand cuff you and told you that you were hard to find. You ask how did they find you and they never told you. They were mad at the fact that one of the girls that was in the office at the front desk knew who I was but did not tell them where I was. Her mother was the one who told me to go to the back through her window. They did not know that though. Off Atlanta which is 4 hours away. You tried to get the information on how they find you. They just said you was not an easy catch but they got you. You arrive in Atlanta bus station. The on bounty that was with the said she is not taking you all the way to New Jersey for $1,500and if the one guy wanted to do so, go ahead. She was leaving and her advice to him was if he don't want to take you, to let you go right there. You said yes leave you there because you knew that your aunt lived 2 hours away in Stone Mountain. The guy got on the phone with his supervisor. He told him he would give him the whole $3,000 if he was to bring you. The result was he was taking you. Hand cuffed all the way there. Long trip in cuffs. One you got there you arrived in Philly where another bounty was to pick you up then return you to the county. You return to the county dark as hell. Time to get it started. You fought it and wine up getting the 20 bundles thrown out because by law if I did go in the house after making a transaction and the drugs that they found was in plain view they are allowed to seize it but if their was no one else in the home and it is 2 officers there one has to keep me detained and the other has to go get a warrant. Being as though they did not do so it got obtain illegally. All what they said I did was a lie. They were looking for some one else stombled across so drugs and pinned it on you with a made up story thinking people would believe them. In New Jersey you are guilty and have to prove your innocents. Crazy. You took the 6 bags they claim they say you with. Another lie bu you had time in a took the deal. 3with a madatory 1 year eligibility of parole. Back down to prison you go. This time when you get to CRAF to see classification they tell you to go down Mountainview Correctional Facility. Annadale is what everybody calls it because of where it is located. Fine lets go. You finally get shipped and once you get there it is all cottages. No cells. Open for all fights a thieves. You play your roll because they give you full minimum status so you going out to the camps that they have. Sweet. You get shipped to the camps the same day. You get there and they are totally different from the ones you been in at Yardville. They are more open. They have the weight pile in the middle of the two camps with the basketball court and you could be outside all day between counts. So you did what do best, adapt and workout. You get put on a tier where there is mostly gang members in but you being you, you fit right in. The days go on as you unpack and get aquinted with the fellow inmates. Everybody cool in your eyes. The days go on and you find your way into the weight pile. Have to group up with the people of your weight class or bigger. You decide to go with the one in your weight class. Your time is getting short and you have no problems yet until you bump into a guy on the court who thought he was bigger and taller tan you. He pushes his weight around on the basketball court so you challenge him to a one on one. He proudly accepts. As the game starts and go on, He start to notice that you are faster than he is and being bigger does not mean anything. He starts to foul more now that he realize that you not just taking him pushing you and backing down. You do what you do and thats push back. It causes a little conflict between you to because now his pride is getting hurt. You are winning the game and the people cheering you on are you bunkies. The system call them gang members but you call them family. As they cheer you on he gets more upset. Brains beat the bronze but without words being exchanged. Now that the game is over you and him are ready to fight. You take it in the wing where it can't be seen by the c/o's. You go down the wing and wait for him. The guys like it how you were the smaller person and you stood up for yourself against the bigger guy and did not care if he had a crew or not. They come down the wing with you and the shortest out the crew said he wanted to fight him and that he got you. You disagreed and they said they wanted him for awhile but couldn't get a reason to so now they do. Thats when you seen that you ran with them. You started thinking about your surrounding and thought that you are with all of them all the time. It is what it is. The guy came down the wing and seen everybody just waiting for him to get there. He got paranoid and talked his way out of it. He never said a word to you the rest of the time there. You now are looked at differently. Like one of them. The next day you in the yard doing pullups and have others on the bar with you. You are now five on a square shaped bar with you on the corner. When you are finished your workout you go to mess and then for the dinner and decide what to eat on your fourth meal of the day. Something was going on on another wing and the people that were involved was on your wing. They came walking fast to you and handed some workout gloves to you and for you to get rid of them and you did. Now you are in with them really. The other people that are on other wings did not mess with you and the c/o's was keeping an eye on you because you are cool with the guys on your wing who they knew where apart of a family. They now show you things that they don't show everybody. The procedure is the same when up for parole. You get the letter in the mail and have to send it back and this time you get the right address. Also in the mail you get a letter in the mail saying your cousin is in the hospital and is dieing from cancer that has spread and can not be stopped. Your world go to dark mood. One of your favorite cousins in going to die and he is younger than you are. You breakdown in tears knowing that he will pass while you are in there and you will never again get the time to spend with him having fun and to tell him that you love him. Time to see parole. You are still in mourning and the result of parole you don't care for. You get called in and to sit on the chair while they say what they feel as though needs to be said. They ask you how do you feel and do you feel like you have changed. You attempt to explain that you have changed and just wanted to get out but the thought of your cousins passing upset you and you cut the conversation short. They see the emotions on your face and ask you to leave the room and to sit on the outside so they can go over what they think is best. At this time it really don't matter. You sit their holding back the tears. They call you back in and they explain their decision. They decided to grant you parole. You was happy but confused because you did not really give a good explaination on why they should let you out. They gave you a few green sheets and explain the obligations of your parole. You get excorted back to your housing unit still shocked at the fact that they let you out on parole. You it settle in as the rest of the guys congradulate you on you going home. Their are a few people on your wing that is leaving around the same time. It was one Damu on the tier who was older than you and could sing real good. He had something waiting for him once he get out and once you get out to hit him up because he will be leaving first. He never been to Atlantic City because he was from Newark and all his fun was in New York. The days wine down and you go even harder in the weight pile. You already bigger than you have ever been. Weighing in at 165lbs. Really look good on you. The day come to you getting out and you are excited. Ready to see your mom and show how big you are. You pack the rest of your things as they call your name to leave. You tell everyone that you was cool with that you will get up with them and that everyone who is still behind once they get out to hit you up. You now have to say your name and number to be released and wait for a van to take you to the train station. They tell you how to get home because they now have a new railway that go from Trenton to Camden. Its funny how things get torn down and other things rebuilt once you are away for awhile. You get on the train from Newark to Trenton. Then from Trenton to Camden and from there you will walk. Show off your weight and to see who is still out and alive. You stroll through fast because you said you will see all that you will see later. You have to see your mom and then go to parole and let them know you are out. You are greeted with hugs and everybody on the block is outside. Fun Day!! Your man who bailed you out is now locked up for murder and his two brothers are also locked up for two murders and an attempt murder. He left the block to you to do what you do as far as the dope game. You can either rent it out to some one and collect the rent money or you can put your own work out there. You meet up with his mother and she breaks it all down to you in who got what on the block. She says to take it slow and see because you just got out. You didn't want to jump head first back into the game so you fell back. You play the park to see who out with his mom and she breaks it all down to you again about whats been going on on the streets as far as the people. Who died, went to jail, who is pregnant by who, and who got issues all the way around the board. You spot this italian woman that worked there. She eyed you knowing she never seen you before. You ask questions like who is she and what do she do. She says that she works their as a coordinator and she married and her husband beats on her. You wanted to know her anyway. You made it your duty to go to the park every chance you get. The friendship with your boys mom started to become distant because you was on parole and you had to get a job. Your thoughts were now on her because she is a new face. Your relationship with your ex distant as well because she meet somebody else she began a relationship with while you were away and on the run in Georgia. You now catch your new eye candy a lot on your days off and after work but only for a short period of time. You two bond together on the low because you both was interested in each other. She had issues going on inside of her marriage along with the children. Your conversations between each other were getting deeper than you both thought so you thought. Manipulation is an evil thing when used in the wrong way... One day it was time for her to get off work and you just happen to show up and the husband was not in the park with her. You both was inside of the trailer where all the paperwork is done at along with meetings. Her husband pops out of know where and assumed we was doing something. I walked out the trailer to sit on the bench when I noticed she was crying and asking for help. He put his hands on her like he always did when he wanted something to go his way and plant fear in a person. He left and she called the cops to get him arrested for assault on a female. They come a locks him up. That very same night you stayed with her and never left. A week goes by and they let him out. He then realizes that you have moved in and he is no longer welcomed. He felt some type of way because for the first time he thinks he can no longer have her and he have to do for him self and can no longer take her money every time she gets paid. Now you are playing step pops to all four of her kids. They felt comfortable with it because they no longer has to live in a house where they have to live in fear. Every morning you would walk with two youngest ones to school and he would be waiting every day. Waiting. Not because he wanted to be there for them but to show you that he is not going anywhere and he will do all he can to break you two up. It only frustrates you and now everyday you have to battle with him. Even after school he would be around making things hard for you. One day you decided enough was enough. He was at the complex with his friends waiting for you to show up to attempt to get in. You went and got your friends. This fight will be his last. Thats what you had in your head. So you was going to bring the pain to him like he was attempting to inflict on you. Once you and your friends get there your mom pull up and blow your cover. How she knew what you were doing you don't know but by the time dude seen what was coming to him it was to late. It kind of calm things down but only another situation happened at night with a different person. You all were sleep one night until you heard commotiotn at your front door like someone was trying to forcefully get in. You turn on the light and they stopped doing what they were doing. You look out the peep hole and seen two people and one had a gun. You said what did they want and who were they looking for. Maybe they had the wrong apartment number. They did not and they wee looking for your girlfriend. You ask why and he did not want to say. You were curious and wanted to know why they were there at that time at night and why haven't you seen them before. They did not want to answer your questions and wanted to speak with her. You said no and that only made things worst. They were drunk. Your girlfriend calls the police and they come. They are escorted out of the building but you knew that it wasn't the last time you would see them. That morning you all wake up and you demanded to know why they were there and who is he really. She cries and says that she had dealing with him before and she don't know why he popped up that day. Later that day he by himself came back to the complex. This time you was not there. You was around your mothers house and seen them two outside talking. You walks up to him and he explains what he is doing there. The littlest daughter was his but she was telling her husband she was his. Now you know why he treated her different. He had thoughts that she wasn't his but the reason why he thought that was because she did not look like him. You was like just because a child don't have your features does not mean the child is not yours. They could have your gens but the child may look like the mother. Ignorance. She finally confesses that the child is his and she cheated inside of there relationship because her husband was cheating its just she got pregnant and said it was her husbands. Crazy. Time go lapse as you work and maintain your work epitics. She presents that her mother wants to see her in another state. You cool with it because you have to work and go with your parole obligations. She go for two weeks and you okay with it. She calls back and forth saying how her stay is. She comes back with exciting news. You can come down there and have a job and a apartment. You go with it. You have gang parole and they are tight with the security. You get involved with your son because your girlfriends daughter is in the same class as your son and she likes him. The problems that you have with the fathers daughter is easing along. Your girlfriend says she wants to go back down there and want to take you with her to meet the parents and the set up that he has if you all was to go and live down there. You was like cool because the part that she has been to, you have not been there before. She is now pregnant with triplets as she say. (huh) You and your family set up a surprise baby shower in the morning. It was nice. You had a cam corder and she did not know what was going on. All she knew was that you both was going over your moms house for breakfast. Surprise as she opens up the door. Very excited she opens up the door. Wow presents for three. She shed tears of enjoyment but the shocker has yet to come. The day went on good as well as the night. The following day she claims to receive a phone call saying that it would be nice for her to come back to Florida and her parents was going to pay the way. You went with the flow skeptical on why she going down there again and she has to work. You ask no questions. She goes down there with the kids this time so her parents can see the kids. She goes and you wish her a farewell off. Days than past and you get a disturbing phone call. It is your girlfriend crying saying she lost all three of the babies. You ask how. She says she fell going up the steps. You say to yourself that it funny how could she lose all three in a simple fall up the steps. You calm her down and say you was sorry and you just want her to come back in one piece. Now you have to tell the family about what happened and that all that was bought had to now be given away or taken back. Crazy how life takes a turn. Your cousin is having a baby as well so he gets most of the things. The days go on and your mind starts to wonder and attempt to figure out, how the hell she lose all three at once. She claims she has a brain anurisum and she did not want to talk about it to much and she use to have fall outs and you would have to bring her back to normal after she becomes conccions. It hurts you to know that one day she will no longer be here and you would be the one to take care of all the kids. She comes back from Florida with all the weight she gained from the babies gone. You are now dealing with a lot at your age and ask your mother for advice. She gives you the best she can and also curious about things now. She ask you did you ever go to any doctor appointments with her being pregnant and with the brain thing. You answer her with a no but she then tells you something is not right. You then start to ask your girlfriend questions about the x-rays you find in the closet pertaining to head head. You explain to her that her that you have aunts who work at a hospital and they have connect with doctors that can help explain things to her if she does not understand and if she needs help with anything. She gets very defensive and attempt to explain all what is going on and why she is so defensive. She does not want to scare the kids in thinking that they will lose their mother so you keep your mouth closed even though it does not sound right. You aunt says the same thing. Something is not right. With the love you have for her you block out all things and just want to move on. The family looks at you crazy like you are just accepting anything she says. True or not. Love can be blind. You just drop the entire situation and just focus on staying on the right path because you are on parole. Gang unit at that. Months past and now she is saying that you all should take a trip down to Florida so you can see if you liked it down there and if you liked it that would be a good move once you get off parole. Yeah so you thought. Parole came around and told you that you have two months left and you did not have to see them until September than again in October. At that time you will sign your max out papers. Cool. You thought you could go to Florida for two weeks then come back to see parole. Then go back down there if you liked it and seek employment. You pack you things to go for two weeks. Staying st her mothers house just for a vacation. You go leaving all things expecting to come back. Yeah you thought. You went on the Greyhound. It was a nice trip with all the kids. You had money so the trip was okay. On the way down there she confessed about who she called mom. The entire time she had you thinking that her actual mother was dead and the person she called mom was actually her grandmother. Her actual mother is where you all were going to be staying along with her step father. The one that actually was there for her when she was growing up. Truth is now coming out about her family. She did not think you would last that long but you did. You get there and what all she said about her sister and her relationship actually is as well. Mostly everything she told you about her family was a lie. You do what you do and that's go with the flow. You get situated and found out that they drink every night. You fit right in. Your girlfriend had different intentions. Her whole plans was to get you to stay down there. You did not know that the kids started school down there in August and her mother said it would be nice if they enrolled in school down there. It was conveicing enough that it would be a smart move to do that if you was thinking about staying. You agreed. It goes all with the plan in staying down there. The only one that would be doing the traveling would be you. There plan was in play but you did not know it. Manipulation remember. Your intentions is to come up but you did not. You stayed down there. Why did you do that you don't know, you do not know. You tell your mom to clear out the apartment how ever she feel. All the furniture keep amongst your inner family and if you was to come back it is only for your clothes or just keep the clothes and give your sister and whoever else help clear it out, to do so. Now you are on the run from parole and they do not know where you are. You start to do you. Do what you do as a father to your kids that you took in and an abused girlfriend. Just so happen their is an opening in the field that you went to high school for. Carpentry/Framing. Good because they are willing to drop you off at the mall where you would be picked up for work with a Framing company.

The father take you shopping for tools that you will need for work. He works at a hospital as the lawn care superviser. You jump right into play with the work field. You meet your boss at the stop. He is the one that is going to be picking you up and dropping you off until you get on your feet. The thing about your boss was that he smoked weed. What! You all the way in there. Not going back to New Jersey for you until they catch up to you. The entire time you are down there, you create 2 bank accounts with a 4bdrm apartment 11/2 bath with the parking in the back of the complex where you can pull your car in and stumble your way into the house. Before all this come into play you go through some awlful 4 weeks in your life living with parents and your family of 4 plus you and your girlfriend. All in a 2bdrm apartment. The complex was nice with a pool gym and luandry hookup. They had the washer dryer in their apartment so you were cool. The nights at the house was crazy every night is different. Either in the a resturant or in the house. One day the mother, step father and you both went to Olive Garden and the mother pulled off her underware and put them on top of her husbands head and they were orange. So embaressed you walked outside. Your girlfriend comes outside after you and apologize for the inconvience. All are outside now and get into the car and go home. The party not over. The drinks continue in the house and the night end crazy. Next day they don't remember. Everyday different for the next month. Now that that apartment came through and you all are moving out they want to be nice. You start buying things and you do the move in thing. Money coming in from work and you feeling good. Every week you check look good. You plan every weekend like it was it was a party every night. Fridays is the kids go out to the mall and enjoy fun with there friends with the money that you have gave them. You and your girlfriend go to a resturant and eat and make happy hour. Satuday was the family out day out and it was fun for all. Anything goes. Beach, park, walks, shopping. You did the works on those days. Sunday was family in the house night. Recovery from a long night. Sleep in and you would cook for the family and the night ended with board games. Family feud was the best dvd game. The weekends went like that all the time. Every Friday you would buy a quater of weed. Life was good until one night out. You were at the bar like a normal night out on the weekend. Out at the resturant another event happened and you walks out drunk. Threw your phone in the street and decided to walk home. Your apartment was not to far away and you were wobbling all the way home. You were so frustrated that it did not matter how you was walking home. A block away from your house the police pulled up on you saying they got a call saying that someone was walking the streets drunk and down in Florida they do not allow people to walk the streets like that. What they do is take you in for a eight hour delox in a cell and let you go from the precient. You told them that you live right up the street and all you could do is continue walking home and they can follow you. They wanted to run your name anyway and the story that you are telling them could be a lie. You think of the fugitive warrant that may pop up out of New Jersey and attempted to talk your way out of it. You could not. The call came back over the radio and the officer ask them to repeat it again. A thought came in your mind to run but you were drunk and you would not get far. The call came back again and this time the one officer took a step back. He with drew his weapon and said for you to put your hands on top of your head. A call came back that you are wanted and could be armed. OMG. You comply and get handcuffed and you go off to jail with no way to get out. You have to see the judge in the morning. You wait over night and your name is called. You see the judge on a t.v. screen and on the other t.v. you can see your girlfriend wondering whats going on. She was crying as the judge tell you that they are holding you for 30 days and if New Jersey does not come get you the have no choice but to let you go. Cool you thought. You go back to your cell with a fight. The officers attempt to grab you and you resist. A little altercation occur but you then give in. Jail mode. There jail is sweet. The people can bring you white under clothes and cocks to where. Your girlfriend did the same but what you did not know was that she was partying with the money you have in the bank. Her name is the secondary on them. You adapt as usual and get into the chess game. You play them on the tier and beat most of them. The 30th day come and your name gets called in the morning. You thought you were being released but the bounties were waiting for you downstairs. They say you can not take your things with you and you were being excorted back to New Jersey for a violation. You have 30 days in on a 62 day run. You get cuffed and you are off to the airport. You are embaressed because you are walking through the airport with handcuffs on and the kids are looking at you like you are hold criminal. Well you was but not like they see on television. They put a coat over your hands but the legs they can not do anything about. They get something to eat and for the first time you get what they call a gyro from Taco Bell. It was good and it was the last meal you had before you start eating prison food. You never flew on a plane before and you had to get on a smaller plane before you can get on a commercial plane. You never flew on either before. First time for everything. The experience was cool. You got to know the difference between flying above and below the clouds. Below the clouds is like a roller coaster and above the clouds is smooth sailing. You get to Philadelphia and they get handed over to the bounties from New Jersey. Then off to CRAF. No stops. You get in there and the same procedure. Strip down and all. You get situated and find out that you only had to do the rest of you time and no running time. That's cool to. You do the remainder 32 days there. You became the runner and now you have the connects to some cigerettes. You are now smoking and eating street food in the middle of the night. You workout until your time is up. The letters from your girlfriend start to slow down until it was time for you to leave. You had a plane ticket waiting for you at the airport and all you had to do was make it there. They let you go and the things that you had as far as cosmetics you left with a friend from the streets as he was coming in. You have a little bit of pull. You leave feeling free. Time to party so you thought. You go straight to the train station and over Philly you go. You did not see your mother or anything. You get to the airport finally and you hear your name called over the speaker to pick up the phone. You pick it up and it was your girlfriend telling you she thinks it would be best if you was to stay at your mother house. You tell her no and that your where coming back home and that your job and all was still there along with your clothes and other things you may need that is important to you. You jump on the plane back. You are curious why she was saying that but you like you time and its time to have fun again. You have a flight to Tampa where a bus ticket she claims was waiting for you. So she said. You get to Tampa and had to walk five hours to a bus station that you did not know where it was. You was just walking following signs hoping you would find bus on the streets. Night fall and you finally see a bus you follow it with your eyes and arrive at a bus terminal only for them to say their is no ticket waiting for you in their system. Wow. Another lie. You stayed at that bus station for more than 24hrs. It was one of the craziest experience you went through in your life. You was calling your house and she was saying the ticket was there and it was not. Finally your name popped in the computer and you wait for the bus. People that was in the station gave you something to eat because you did not have any money. You get on the bus relaxed waiting to arrive. The weather is nice and you are ready to enjoy life. You arrive there and you decided to walk home. She was not there went you got there. You had a tree in front your house where you can climb it and jump on the roof to open the front window that you had a fan in. You push the fan in and open up the screen You are breaking into your own house. You got in the room only to find a duffle back with men clothing and blunt guts in the bag. The bag was not yours. You check the closet to see if your clothes was in there and they was. You also check the drawers to see if all your bank check books was there and all that have been written in your name. Surprised what you find out. She have been writing checks with no money was in the account. You find empty beer bottles under the couch and blunt guts in the trash can. She was partying all on your expenseses and you did not know about it. Your bills was backed up and all the money was spent and gone while you were away. You wait for her to get home. She does not come home til around 8:30 p.m. She in surprised you were in the house. The kids were happy to see you but she was in the state of shock because she had other things going on. You wanted to hear the reason why it was a duffle bag of clothes in the bedroom. She waited by the door and could not answer the questions you presented to her and you heard a knock at the door. Twice it sounded off. She did not answer. It sounded off again. At this time you was about to jump and get to the door but she opened it up just a little bit to say you were there and she shut it. You jump up and push her out the way and opened the door. All you seen was a guy getting into a car and pulling off. You slam the door and commence to hitting her but you held back. You had to gather your thoughts on all that is going on and what was going on while you were gone. You ended the night like welcome home. You had sex and you thought you were the only one in had been in it but after what just happen and the bag, yes she have been touched. You go with it demanding answers in the morning. You also get on the phone to call your boss to let him know you are out and you are ready to go back to work. At this time you simi forgave her because a lot was on the line as far as financies that you had to get back. You worked and paid as much as you can. The company that you was apart of was starting to go downhill because of personal issues. It was splitting up and you had to do something. She convenced you that it was best to move on to something else through a temperary service and. You did it and had problems with trust issues in the home big time. You hook up with the Masonic brothers and get accepted into the temple. You take on your degrees as a mason into the Master Mason degree. Your relationship has calmed down and you get back on board with land a framing position through the temp. Service that you went to everyday. Your patterned became known to your girlfriend and she started to do her again. Once again manipulation from a female to a male is very hurtful. Even more hurtful when the guy is doing nothing but right. You caught her in another act and this time it is with the same guy. You came home early one day and he was in the house. You like just when things you thought was about to get right she messes them up again. He afraid to come outside. You do not know if his car is parked on the back or the front. To the right of your apartment is a one bedroom apartment that has a ramp for the elderly man that stay next door. So all is open along with a walk way the the back of the complex to the parking lot and walk path in case people don't want to walk in the front of the complex. Nice little play area for kids to play and ride bikes and get into trouble but calm. You could hang your clothes in the back. He yells out he was just coming to tell her it is all over and he does not want any trouble. You more mad with her if anything. You on the porch and one of the daughters is now trying to get in. She runs back and forth outside and you hoping to catch a door open. You get upset and know that it maybe a messed up ending and it is really not his fault because he is misled on like you are and you know that but not him. So you don't blame him. He finally comes out and all that is going in your head is that you are going to pack your things and go. You go in to the house after he gets into his car then leave. You go in the house upset and getting ready to pack your things before she fell out in the kitchen. You go to her rescure but this time you look over her thinking she is faking. Thinking she just that because of what happened. You grabbed a beer out of the refriedgerator and then attempted to revive her. She comes around and in your mind if she was faking she would have said something about what you did. She plays along and when she claims she is fully concience she says she know you walked over her. You deny it because if she was unconconcious she would not have known that. She leaves it alone and you go on with the day. You feeling guilty of the kids not having a mother and for no child have to go through something like that you stay. The brothers from the lodge likes your knowledge and the fact that you are young in their eyes to possess that kind of wisdom. They do fish fries on every Friday and they like that you are energetic and want to see the lodge grow and one day you become the grand master of the lodge. One day your mom tells you that she owes her $2,000 and you ask why. She explains that while you were away she was saying that you was calling her on collect and telling her to call your mother and ask for help with paying the bills which was a lie. Now it is on you say. Its one thing to do something to you and it is another to do it to your mother. The arguments start because she is saying your mother is a liar and she don't owe her anything. Your mother is saying that she can mail you all the western unions she used to send the money to her. You attempted to drop it but decided to leave because everyday it is something that was once told to be true all a lie and somethings did not even come out yet. You pack up and leave and you make it all the way to Jacksonville, FL. Until you were at a layover and she managed to make her way there to stop you from getting on the bus. At that moment you said to yourself if a female or male is willing to travel hours so they can stop you from going any further that's love. As usual she convents you to stay. You all find a way to get back home by writing a check to a cab company that they could not cash until the following day and only to hear that the account is closed. You had to find a way to get you all home. She came with the kids. You make it home and everybody is tired. You tell her that since it is her fault for all of this you want her to unpack your things and put them away and she did so. The days went on regularly. The love was gone and the trust was definetly out the window. You was walking away from a lot and you were walking away from the kids and that is not what you wanted. You dealt with it all. NO more fun and games like it used to be. Dull moments now are the everyday thing. Her plans was to get out of dept with your help and do what she came down there to do and that's do her. One rainy day something just did not seem right. You immediately thought she was doing her and it was time for you to show her son before you walk out of their lives for a little bit. You csll her on the phone and tells her to come to the house that it important and and she had to come quick. You hang up and tells him if a guy come running out of the friends house before her thats who she is cheating on you with. It did not happen and he did not believe you. So you call again and say the same thing and hang up and for sure a guy came out of the house and she come out not to long after him. Now he is a believer. He is ad because he knows you are going to leave. She was in the state of shock when she came through the door out of the rain> You tried hard to not hit her. A argument went on and you left it as that. It was Sunday the next day and she claims she had to go to church. You said okay and watched her and one of the daughters walk down the street. Once out of your sight you rush back inside to pack your things and explain to her son all whats happening but he already knew. You tell him to take care of his mothers and be the man of the house. He walks with you to the bus stop and wait for the bus with you. You tell him to protect his mother and to keep in touch with you. The bus come and he sheds tears. You tell him you love him and you get onto the bus and away you go. No turning back this time. You take the long trip and arrive back in Camden 27 hours later and your mother is waiting for you. You greet her with a hug and of to the house you go. It is night time so it is time to sleep. No one knows you are back but your mom. The phone rang and you pick it up. It was child support asking to speak to you. You was shocked because no one knew you were home so why would child support be calling looking for you. They say that they got a message that you were back in town and they have been trying to get in contact with you about making a payment. You could not respond but say you will have some money for them until Friday and they are telling you if you do not have it by Friday a warrant will be out for your arrest. You just agreed and hung up the phone. Now you have to cone up with a thousand dollars by Friday and it is Monday and you don't have any income to present anything close to that. You just came back from Florida, Like what is going on. You just waking up. You knew you would have to answer them sooner than later. It is what it is. Time to see what all was going on while you were away for 3 1/2 years. You take a shower the usual every day thing. You pop out of the house when all the neighbors are out on there porches. Its the summertime so everybody is outside. Who all is outside is glad to see you all healthy. Its still early and some are at work. You for the first time see that you are not use to being without your now ex-girlfriend. You have in your head that with the right phone conversation with her you would go back. You also realized that you looked at females different. You despised them and if you was to mess around with another females it will be just to get yourself something to easy your sexual desire than you are gone. You are not a womanizer but you think that all females have different intentions and you would no longer allow yourself to feel for a woman again. It wam bam thank you mam and keep it moving. You also have the problem that you had to come up with the money to pay child support in which you don't have. Your father and mother wine up coming through for you and paid it off for you so you can have a better start. Your mother seen that you was asking questions like it was your fault like you did something wrong. She explains to you that it is not your fault and she had just the remedy to cheer you up. She introduce you to what they called a Cabarate. You asked what that was. She says its a once a month thing when a party bash was being thrown and it is for the grown and sexy. It is also bring your own bottle. Hell you up for it. You like having fun and love to dance. Its a family thing. Once you get dressed to impress and go get a bottle of liquor and some beer and you are off to the party. Adult gathering. Once you got their you seen that their are grown and sexy out to have a good time with old school music and what was being worn was amazing. People was coming in fur coats, cat sits, gator shoes, the works. This is you. Getting on the dance floor is surely what you needed. You mother was right again as she always is. You got drunk and had a good time. You were breaking out of your mold a little now. Your weight was up because you was working out when you were in Florida. You wine up getting a job that our mom helped you with and you were on your way. You met a female going to the liquor store one day and thought you could not get her attention. She was sitting on the porch waiting for her ride to come pick her up. While she waited you went to the store and brought her a bottle to drink and you gave her your number to call. You did not think she would call you but she did that night but you were so drunk that you did not hear the phone ring. Th following morning you returned her call and thought it would be nice to hang out one day. Your sister and brother in law moves in with your mother, brother, and you. House full now but you are cool with that because you miss your sister and you wee real cool with your brother in law. He is a fly dude. Grown but wild. Did not play the stupid stuff but was down in every way. He was grown before his time. You liked him. A good hand out partner as well. Late nights you both are on the porch smoking weed before the night end for you both. Your mother did not allow smoking going on in the house. She did not smoke anything. You had a couch on the porch everybody who came to see yall would have the couch to sit on when all was outside. They had a Honda with two 15inch speakers in the trunk with 4 EV's of 8inch speakers going across the top of the back seats and 2 amps to hold the bass and voice that was coming from them. Their system was loud. As the days go on and you are now working and the friendship that you have developed with the female friend that gave you her phone number is getting serious. You both are Virgos. Crazy combination but it worked. You both was alike and she filled that void that you had in your heart. One night you asked your sister to borrow the car to go down the street to pick up Chinese food for you that you ordered. She says yes and you turn on the tunes and started blasting the music when you got a phone call from the female friend. You go pick her up get her some food and go to the liquor store. You stayed out past the time your sister gave you to go to the store. You find yourself at the waterfront enjoying the night sky and water with your friend. It get tends and your phone is ringing. Your sister is mad that you was not home yet and you were doing other things than what you asked her for the car to do. It one thing you knew and that was not to piss off your sister. That was a no go. You come back to the house with the female friend and your brother in law is on the porch smoking a cigg. He says your sis is pissed at your but you are now typsy and you are just like she got her car back and now you about to have one more fun with the female that you brung home. The ending of the night was cool and you started a relationship with her. You thought it was a good step in the right direction to recovery. It turned out to be a good move for you. Every Friday you got paid you would buy a bottle of Greygoose that started off you and you new girlfriend and it would end however. Your girlfriend did not have a job but she played her part to the fullest. You start to realize that not all female are the same. Some just want to be loved as well. One day the drinking got out of control. You were at her mothers house when you phone goes off. It was another female. She decided to text you and you text back. Your girlfriend goes to the bathroom and you get another text. She wants to hang out but you could not do so because you were with your girlfriend. She come down and ask why your phone keep going off. You play it off and say it was your mother. She half believe you. She plays it off and act like she had to use the bathroom again. Then she snuck down and caught you on the the phone you jump and she asked you who is that. You go to the kichen and put the the phone in the sink. She hurry up to pick it out. She then runs in the basement to see what you were doing. She sees the messages and flips out on you. She slams the phone because you were lieing and as you attempt to grab all the pieces she punch you in the face. You grab her and attempt to restrain her but she some how come up with this strength and slams you on the floor like she was in the WWF. Her son comes to the top of the steps and sees all. You then try to go up the steps so you can leave. She is fighting with you all the way out the door but don't want you to leave at the same time. You finally get out the door and you fall backwards down four flights of stairs. You get up mad then go after her. You both go over the rail the seperates the two houses. You get up and go all the way home pissed. You tell your sister what happened and she goes around their but do nothing because she knows how you two are. You and her both walk back around the corner home. You go to bed but wake up in pain. You go around her house and apoligize for your actions and hug her as she is in pain as well. You both try to make it all up but the fight was the end of the relationship. Time goes on but she is still your friend and you check on her from time to time. Yall hit it off a couple times but it would go no further than that. You get fired from your job and now you need a steady income so you start selling weed on the block. It started slow but then pick up. Your mother do not know whats going on because she is staying at her boyfriends house every night. You started messing with this female that your cousin was going out with her cousin. Everything was going good. You had a cover up for if your mother was to come by, but for the most part you are moving how you are suppose to move. The block started going good and some additional things was to be put out on to the block. That was going good but people would shut down the block at an early time to avoid the attention. Every time they close shop people still come look for it so you decided to keep a little for those reasons. That was picking up along with your product until one night it all got cut short. You do the normal with putting things away before going to bed and start enjoying the night with drinks and something to smoke with your new girlfriend. You put the money under books and the product where ever you decide to put it. In the morning your peoples come over to pick up the money. You go to the books and find that the money that you had put there is no longer there. Your girlfriend claims she did not take it but you two were the only ones in the house at the time. You come out of the pocket for it. It was a set back for you. You took her home and decided not to mess with her any longer. All she had to do ask you for some money but instead she choose to be disloyal. The women that you choose to wife. You stayed single for a little bit and your hustle was up. Another situation came about when several bundles of dope came up messing and the two people that were involved was you and your cousin. He claim he gave you the bundles last night to get rid of and you were saying that you gave them back to him because he came back to the block to get them before he when to sleep. You both was high out of your minds and he does not remember. They relied on him and said that you had to pay it. They looked it like you have the money anyway and you could pay it. You did but you were upset. You slipped but it won't be the last. They demanded you pay it back and as you know you not paying anything because it was not your fault. If anything you pay half and the other half take up with the other person. Days go past and an attempt was made but you still did not give in. One night goons was coming for you masked up and they caught you slipping again but this time the event did not happen because of a true friend that send what was going down and stopped them. With the respect of him they did nothing. You just left the block because it was not worth it. You just know who your friends, family, and foes are. You go to your grandmothers house again to start over but don't know how. You started hanging with your peoples and their sons and you managed to work your way back into the dope game. The youngest one had at least a thousand dollars put up. You thought it was your time. A dude got locked up on the block and other people did not want to open it back up. You took that opportunity to go in and you did. You finished out that night and was asked did you wasn't to come back the next morning. Of course. Full time this time and you was not leaving it this time until you felt as though you were on top but that never happens. You start to put in work on the block and the money was pilling up. They loved the way you hustled and was not scared to take chances. You met a female that did not speak English hey you were in their. She was independent and had her own hustle. She was straight from Puerto Rico. Around your age and only had three kids and doing good for herself. Her older sister lived with her but she was cool. They were cool and expected you in as a friend but you manage to work through that as well. People started seeing you more and more at her house. Every night when she cooked she made sure you had a plate. On or off the block. You called her your girlfriend and gave her a nickname. She liked it but was raised to not exit her race to date or have any children out of her race. The old way of teaching. She liked the attention you would give her but said you were a close friend to her and that she had an open space for her baby dad if he got his stuff together. You respected that. You were still their for her more than he was and everybody heard you call her girlfriend. One day she got a phone call from her family from PR. They said her father had past away. She cried hard and did not know what to do about going over there because she did not have that kind of money to get there. You had money so you offered to pay for her plan ticket. You both became closer because in her time of need and all the people around flashing money could not help her but you did. You knew you were going to make it up over the next couple of days so you did not care as long as you seen her see her father off that was okay with you. Back to the block hard. A week goes past and she comes back. She has lost weight like she has not eaten but she looks good and she liked the new look. She vow to pay you back but you did not want it. She said anything you needed to get done she got you. You tried her one day. You were making so much money one day on the block that you called her son to come get some money so he could take to her to put up for you. She did so and at the end of the night you left her with the money. You did not want to walk home with that much money on you. The next morning you go to her and she shows you the money she had put up for you. You told her to hold it and at the end of the night you will come get it. It was times you stayed on the block from 6 a.m. to 11 p.m Dope Boy. You go to her at the end of the shift and she gives you the money. You never counted it. You chilled for a little bit because it was the weekend then you went home. The next morning you did not go to the block. You was going to do the 3 p.m to 11 p.m shift. She gave you the rest of the money. She had it seperated in to different spots because she did not want to mixed her money with your money. You trusted her from then out. Anything she needed she got hands down. One day you were on the block and it was your peoples birthday on the block you hustled on. You were in the spot light now so you wanted to show them that you can dance to spanish music. Yes you showed your ass that night. You went home got changed and came back with a bottle for the party. Like they did not have any. You was on that night. It was a good night and you danced your ass off. You ended up at your female friends house. Don't know how you got there but you was. You woke up in your own urine. You was so passed out that you did not wake up to use it. You was so embaressed that you did not wake her. You just gave her a kiss on her forehead and left.

Crazy night ending in a bad situation. The first though. Back to the block and you was not going to see her in a couple of days. You finally popped up and the situation did not change to two relationship as friends. She was drunk to and she did not remember what she did that night neither. All that time you wanted to stay at her house with her one night. You finally did and look what happened. Blame it on the alcohol. Funny. One day it all came to and end. You knew that being on the block so much one day your day will come to face the law. They ran down on all of yall on the block from all directions. They found your stash and being as though you had the most money on you, you wore it. Back to the county you go but you was not mad at all. You were tired off all the long days and nights. No sleep sometimes and sleeping on the couch was wearing you out. You get in the county and your weight is in the basement. Your skin color is dark. You look crazy. Time to get it in order. You was going to wait for your discovery because there was no way you could have gotten caught red handed. You sat and you worked out. You knew you were going to be there for awhile and you wanted a runners job. You land one and from there you took over all 3 shifts as a runner. Anything that comes through there has to come through you first. You locked it down so everybody can eat. You met somebody that was very strong mentally. He caught your attention. You found out somethings about him that you knew a little about but more than the next and you got accepted into the family. New start for you in your life. They move him to another tier because they bring up a new charge on him. The put him right next door and the communication only got closer. As the time went on you became the runner and you were fighting your case. At the end you took a 364 with 2 year probation. You already had a year in so you went home later that day. Your mother was expecting you. You picked up a lot of weight over that year and your mother liked how you looked. You had probation on your heels so you had no choice to fly right. You was just happy to be out. You slept the night away and had plans for the next day to see who you needed to see. The next day you went back to the block in which you got looked up on waiting to see old friends and to let them know you did your time like a man. You went to see the man that owned the block and he gave you a couple of dollars. It was not much for that time you did but he respected what you did. You birthday was coming up and as usual your friend mom was first up. It was like a celebration of her birthday and you coming home. This night was different. You dranked and danced. During this time somebody brings boxing gloves around to see who wanted to put on them and friendly box. All that trash people be talking about they can fight nobody wanted to put on the gloves with the person that brung them out to play with. It was a family member and they knew he could box. You laughed because nobody wanted to box so you stepped up. To match started and it was fun until you got hit lightly as you took a step back to dodge the punch. Your back heel hit a brick that was pulled up half way from the ground. You were drunk so you fell backwards and could not catch your fall. You hit the back of your head and knocked you out cold. You went to the hospital with a fractured skull and blood was leaking into your brain and you was in a coma. You were watched day in and day out. You woke up 3 days later on your birthday with the touch of your friends mothers hand. She was there with her daughter and a balloon. You was wondering what you were there for and you did not know what happened and had a big headache. Blessed because if the crack was any bigger you could have died. Thank God first and back on your high hose you go. You signed yourself out and your mother came to get you. The doctors orders was to keep an eye on you because you could fall asleep and not wake up. They gave you 3 pills to take to help with the healing of your skull, for the pain, and to help you sleep. You were healthy because you at good and took care of your body while you were locked up. Believer. You had to see probation and tell them you are on medication and what happened. You probation officer was a female and she looked at you like all the nonbelievers do at people who got in trouble and thing you are a waste of society time and you could not rehabilitate. So you two had a problem. You figure just do what you have to do and she really can't say anything but you can. You working paying fines so you did not care so you started smoking. Every week you had to see her and every week your urine was dirty. She told you that you had to go to a program for the dirty urine. You explain to her you don't need a program and once you get their they will see you don't have a problem. You go just to comply with the orders. They evaluate you and determined that you did not need it. Your p/o was mad. She looking for something to have you locked up. Days go on and you get hired by the company through the temperary service. You made it and now it was time to seek a higher position. You are on your probationary period so you had to take it easy. You were warned that the supervisor has a disrespectful way of talking to people. You know how to deal with people like that. One day you were going to be late so you called the number that was given to you at orientation I case of lateness but what they did not say was th number only fully operate during the day and once the first shift is over all calls that come to that number goes to voice mail. You arrive to work and the supervisor got on you. You try to explain to him about the number but with his nasty attitude he was not hearing it. He told you to go home. You were puzzled about it. You went home mad. The next day you go to work with proof of what you were talking about. You pull him into a room and to tell him about it. He was scared because of your approach so he told you to go home even with the proof. You were really mad and was determine to prove yourself. The next day was Friday pay day and you wanted to come talk with one of the big bosses from the company. He was already aware of the situation between you to. You showed him what was wrong and he believed you but the supervisor said you were high and that is the reason he sent you home. You told him you were not and he told you that you still had your job but you had to take a urine test. You explain to him the only way you and to take a urine after getting hired is if you were in an accident at work. He says that is true but you are in your probationary period and they can kinda do what they feel as though fight but has to have a good reason to do so and he feel this is one. You told him you would go to the lab that day but also showed him you had to be in court at the time you were talking to him. He said that it needed to be done by the end of the work shift. You agreed. You went straight to court. You had to be there because your p/o wanted you locked up. You was in court all day and when you were finished the lab was closed. So you know you lost your job. Another set back. You have bills still you have to pay along with your fines. You did what you normally do when things get rough financially, go to the block. Dope boy. You started off slow but it picked up so you go full time like you not on probation. Crazy. Things were going okay until an incident happened at home with you and your brother. You two fight in which you started but it was the straw that broke the camels back. The cops were called as well as the ambulance. You cut your elbow real bad and had to go get stitches. You get 32 of the and a pair of hand cuffs. The police charge you with assualt. You have one bail but you have a no bail for the violation of probation so you sit. You fight the case and in the end you could not beat the entire thing. And if you would have taken time served after being there for eight months you still would have went to prison because it would have violated it so you just take two 3flats and go upstate. Not mad but ready to get it all over with. The judge gave you all your jail credit but once you got upstate the DOC seperated the time and gave you the least time and had to start from there. Now you are mad. You get to prison and you start your workout plan. You said to yourself that you wee going to come home 200lbs this time. You went down with time in so you had to see parole right away to determine if you were fit to go home. You go through the process and time to see them. You knew it was a possibility that you were not going to get it because every time you get on parole or probation you violate. They grant you parole but you have to go to a program first. Once you complete 6 months of it then you can reside at the approve address. You were at the program for 4 months and then got a job on the street. You got a warehouse job and told those who could go out to look for a job to come to where you were working and they did. At this time everybody was smoking in the program and you were not allowed to. They took random urine testes but what they did not know is its a test that do not pick up specific drug so everyone was getting it in. You was in the wave as well until you came in with a little piece of synthitic weed that you did not know it was there came out of your pocket while getting the change out. The worker said to you what it looked like but it was so small he could have through it in the trash but instead he put it in an zip lock bag and told you to go upstairs. You were drunk a little so you went to sleep. The next day was Saturday and no one was going anywhere unless someone had a job that required you to work that weekend but no one did. The other workers heard what has happened and they were funny about it knowing whats going to happen come Monday. You on the phone with who needed to know. Monday come and you try to leave and go to work, their was a hold on you and you were upset because you did not want to miss work. You had the job readiness lady to make a call for you and the outcome was that you was not to leave the building. You had to answer to the parole people and you knew that could go any way for you. They came and you had to explain how you had it in your pocket. You admit that it did come out of your pocket and how it got their you do not know. They put the cuffs on you anyway. You were going to jail. You sat in the county for 2 days and you got shipped to CRAF to answer to a panel that was only one person who hears your side then takes it back to their supervisor to make a final call. You was there at least a month before seeing anybody. You had all your paperwork on what happened and all incidents that happened while their. It looked good for a minute but the way the papers where written up, you knew you were going back so you settled with it and prepared your self in going back to prison to set the remaining of you state time. You seen classification and they said for you to go to Bayside State Prison. You get down there and you run into you cousin who raps and you peoples that you made friends with while in the program you thought went home and was doing good. It was funny that you all met back in there. Everybody was maxing out. Bayside was nothing like Southwoods State prison. Bayside was hot and if you did not have a fan you was going to burn up. At times you had no choice but to go outside it was hot. You were outside anyway but sometimes you slept in the first yard movement and went outside the next one which was at night. You was behind the wall for a month and a half before seeing classification to get your full minimum status. You all get that status and head out to the camps they have. Depending on your points they give you and the crime with time you have left you get out into the other camps they have based somewhere else. You liked there camps because it had weight outside and the weather was nice. It was the summer time. You all wind up coming to the other camps after being on the compound camps for a month and a half. Their was the place you can go to the halfway house fast if you wanted to. I'm talking about the people would come out and call you to see if you wanted to go there. You had like 3 months to go so all you did was focus on what needed to be done once you went home. You hit the weight pile and had on your mind that you was going to hit that 200lb class. Your bunky was fly as well and his weight was up. He was real cool with the dude that worked at night in the kitchen and you both ate good every night. You had street food every night. You did not really eat off the commissary. He wanted to get you to what you wanted your weight to be and when you did order whatever he needed you got for him. Like cosmetics. Time was winding down and it was time for you to go home. You are 200lbs and you look good. They called your name the night before to pack your things. Maxing out finally. You gave all your food to your bunky and exchanged information and rested the rest of the night ending it with a big feast. The next morning was here and your name was called to eat breakfast. You dressed to impressed and ready to leave. You give your farwells to the ones who showed love to you and you showed your cousin love and know once he touch his time will be. His time to take off in the rap industry. You get your things and go to the front to be processed to leave. Your name gets called and was told you have a ride outside waiting for you. Yes it is your time to shine. Fate is what they call it.......

Printed in the United States
By Bookmasters